Author's Note

Although this novel is inspired by the story of Jephthah from the Bible, it is written as a contemporary Christian romantic suspense and is not intended to be an exact retelling.

JEP

Inspired by the Book of Judges

SHAWNA COLEING

Copyright © 2024 by Shawna Coleing

All rights reserved.

No part of this book may be reproduced in any form or by any electronic or mechanical means, including information storage and retrieval systems, without written permission from the author, except for the use of brief quotations in a book review.

Any references to historical events, real people, or real places are used fictitiously. names, characters, and places are products of the author's imagination

Chapter 1

THE LIGHTS CLINKED and popped as they blinked to life, filling the cold hallway with a jaundiced glow.

Emery hurried down the corridor, hugging the painfully small pile of files to her chest. She had hoped for more evidence. Unless her prayers were answered, these wouldn't be enough.

The fluorescent bulbs continued to light her way at intervals until she reached the exit and climbed out of the archival dungeon that had imprisoned her for the last four hours.

Back in the office, she held her breath as she crossed the nearly empty bullpen to her supervisor's room where she found the door slightly ajar. Clearing her throat, she waited at the threshold.

Sylvia Gardener, whose tight bun emphasized the shape of her square face, looked over the rim of her glasses and smiled. Or it could have been a grimace. Her fingers hovered above the keyboard, unwilling to give up on the email she was writing until she knew the nature of the disruption.

"Is there something I can do for you, Miss Chapman?" Gardener said.

Emery hesitated before taking a step inside. She was always hesitating. As it was, she should have brought the files to Gardener days ago. Now, it might be too late.

"It's about the mission," Emery said.

Gardener relinquished the keyboard, dropping her hands into her lap. "You mean the one the task force is executing as we speak?"

"Yes." Em looked down at her files and almost bit her lip but knew it would look unprofessional.

"Did you have something you wanted to show me?" Gardener said, impatience edging her question.

"If you have time."

"I don't, but you've obviously gone through a lot of trouble." Gardener held out her hand and took possession of the files. "You may as well sit."

Emery did but remained perched on the edge of the chair. "I had some concerns."

"Concerns?"

"Yes."

"About the mission that is in progress as we speak?"

Gardener always made Em repeat herself when she was irritated—as if hoping Em would catch on without an explanation being required. "And you didn't feel like sharing them before now?"

"I should have. But it was more of a gut feeling, so I talked myself out of it."

"What made you talk yourself back into it?" The look that Gardener gave her over her glasses was more of a glare this time.

"I couldn't get it off my mind. I know it's almost too late, but I had to try."

"I hope your interruption means you have more than discomfort to base your concerns on."

Em gave her an apologetic smile. "I hope so too."

Gardener flipped through the first folder. "This is the Bashar file?" She glanced across the first page, then turned several and read for a minute.

"Yes. And Darwish and Bilal. And a few more from before my time here. I couldn't find as much as I'd expected. I, uh…" She almost apologized for wasting Gardener's time and excused herself. "I thought I remembered there being more."

Gardener reached across her desk and picked up a large Hanuman statue she'd brought back from a recent trip to Cambodia. It was poised and ready to strike. She placed it on top of the files, holding them in place.

"Why don't you tell me what's bothering you," Gardener said. "Because from where I'm sitting, there's nothing to constitute any concern beyond a danger level all of those agents are accustomed to and trained for."

"It's not their training I'm worried about. It's the information we received and how it came about. The way the other ops were handled."

"If you have a problem with the team—"

"No. It's not that. I'm not the only one who's found

this entire operation over the last year unusual. We've had so many problems we've never faced before."

"The world is changing. We have to adapt. That's normal."

"And the intel we're receiving? It isn't coming through the usual channels. Everything is so quiet, and then out of nowhere we get this lead."

"You're concerned because we've had a breakthrough? Luck doesn't exist on this task force. Everyone here has been working their butts off to catch these guys. And you know that whenever we get information that may lead us to the truth, it gets taken apart and put back together. We look at everything and weight it up. The assistant director was confident to move on this, and the deputy director agreed. If you believe you know better than them, perhaps you're in the wrong job."

This time, Em did bite her lip. "But we found it so… easily. That's what bothers me."

"I wouldn't call the way we gathered that intel easy. It was messy. Very messy."

"I know. But if you look through the files…or…I was hoping you'd see the connection. There's not much, but it's there."

"Have you considered that you're seeing a ghost because you're desperate to see it? There's nothing in here to support anything you're saying."

"But it was there—" Em jerked straighter in the chair. "—I mean…"

Gardener leaned forward an inch, and her face hardened. "What was there?"

"The information. I remember—"

"Then where has it all gone?"

Emery's mouth remained open as she tried to find a fitting response. "I'm not saying someone removed it."

"I should hope not. Or if you do, you had better bring me something more than a gut feeling."

"No, I know." She squeezed her hands into her lap. "I don't think anyone's done anything with it. I must have remembered wrong. In fact, I've spent the last several hours in the archives proving that I remembered it wrong. I just can't explain how or why. I don't know how I've put together what I have in my head."

"You didn't overhear anyone speaking? The other agents? Lawson?"

"No. I don't like to eavesdrop."

"Then maybe it's like I said. You had a bad feeling, and you had to justify it."

"But what if I'm right? What if our team is heading into a trap? If something happens to them, and I did nothing, I'd never live with myself."

"So, that's what brought you to my door in the end."

"Yes."

Gardener squeezed the bridge of her nose. "Emery, while I appreciate your passion for your job, you are an analyst, not a soothsayer. We need facts, not intuition."

"I know. And I tried to bring you more."

"Even if you found what you were looking for, what course of action could we take?" She looked at her watch. "The operation will likely be over in a few hours."

"We could pull them out."

"You'll definitely need more than this." She tapped

the files. "Without probable cause, there's nothing we can do. There have been countless man-hours put into this. You really think Lawson will call it off because you have a bad feeling?"

Em dropped her eyes to the floor. She was desperate to shake her head and walk away, but she was determined to see this through to the end. "We could try. It would mean more coming from you."

"No offense, but I'm not willing to lose face on your hunch. You're a great analyst, and I like you, but I won't die on your sword."

"No. Of course."

"I'm not trying to hurt your feelings. In a job like this, you can't be thin-skinned."

"I'm not hurt. I completely understand." Em stood. "But I had to try."

"For what it's worth, I know you did your best. You were thorough, as you always are. I wouldn't expect anything less."

"Thank you. I won't take up any more of your time."

"Would you do me a favor?"

"Of course."

"You said you spent hours in the archives. I've been down there. I know what it does to you. All that frustrated searching you've been doing would have blown your fears way out of proportion and twisted you in knots."

"I came out with the same concerns I had going in."

"Be that as it may, I want you to take a walk and clear your head. In a few hours, the team will return, hopefully with more answers. And your fears will be alleviated."

"I'd rather get back to work."

"Then I'm ordering you to take a break. Go get a coffee. It's a beautiful day. Take it in. Refresh. I don't want to see you back here for at least an hour."

Em wanted to protest, but the fight had gone out of her. "Yes, ma'am." Her legs were stiff as she walked to the door.

"Oh, and Em?"

She spun. "Yes?"

Gardener was holding out the files. "Take these with you. I don't envy you putting them back."

"Thanks." She collected the pile and hugged them to her chest again, this time in defeat.

On her way out, she stopped at her desk long enough to drop the files there before walking to the elevator. Her eyes remained locked on the floor until the doors opened, and she looked up to see a man in his early sixties give her a once over because she stood in his way. His lips pursed in their usual frown.

"Assistant director." Em nodded as she shifted sideways to give him room to exit the elevator. "Wait." She quickly added.

"Yes?"

"Uh, it's—uh—the mission. I'm worried about it." She got the words out before she could chicken out. "I think the information we gathered was too easily come by. I'm worried it's a setup."

He crossed his arms. "Aren't you an analyst?"

"Yes, sir."

"I read Gardener's report. I didn't see any issues listed. Not that it's the analyst's job to identify operational concerns."

"No, I've…I've only brought this up now. I wanted to put together more—"

"Have you spoken to Gardener?"

"I have, sir."

"And what did she say? Was she as concerned as you?"

"No, sir. But I believe—"

"How long have you been with us?"

"Over eighteen months."

"Do you know how many successful operations Gardener has been with us for?"

"I don't know, sir, no."

"Seven years' worth. Mostly successful. If you're telling me all you have is conjecture, I will take her conjecture over yours every day of the week."

"I understand, but I—"

He walked away without another word.

It took Em a moment before she could breathe again. No part of the day had gone how she'd expected it to. She jammed her thumb into the elevator call button several times, willing the doors to open so they could swallow her up. When she finally climbed inside, she sighed back against the railing, holding back tears all the way to the first floor. Maybe Gardener was right. Maybe you couldn't have thin skin in this job. But she did. Being an analyst shouldn't require a hard exterior. Some of the information they assessed had details that weren't easy to read, but they were always easy to compartmentalize. Having those you worked with closely dismiss your concerns was much harder. So too was ignoring the gnawing knot in her stomach.

Before the doors opened, she pressed on her face to massage away the emotion and sniffed back what was left.

She smiled tightly at the guards she passed, then hurried out the large glass double doors and down the broad steps to the sidewalk before pulling out her phone.

Lifting her face to the sky to absorb the warmth, she made a call and counted off the rings until it was answered.

"Shouldn't you be working?" the woman on the other end said.

"Hi to you too."

"Don't get me wrong, Em. I love to hear from you, but when you call me during work hours, it freaks me out a little. I'm always the one calling you. So, tell me there is nothing to worry about."

"There is nothing to worry about, Aunt Carla. As I've said before, being an analyst in the Terrorism Task Force isn't dangerous."

"First of all, I have told you a million times to stop calling me 'aunt'. We're all adults now. And second, that's not true. I've seen the movies. I know they can bust in there and shoot the place up."

Em could hear the amusement in her aunt's voice. "If that happens, then I will use my unrealistically impressive movie skills to take them all out by myself."

"Good for you."

"That's not to say I didn't just have the single most

mortifyingly embarrassing encounter of my life. I'm contemplating running away to join a convent. Or a circus. Whichever I can find first."

"We're all idiots now and then. What makes you so special?"

"You don't understand. This is next-level humiliation."

"Did I ever tell you about the time I walked into the wrong classroom—?"

"This is different."

"All right. Tell me what happened. I take it you still have a job?" Carla said with a hint of wariness.

"Barely. You know how you're always saying I should be braver and stick up for myself? Speak up more?"

"Hang on, you're pinning this on me?"

"No, I'm creating context."

"Okay. Continue."

"You say I should stop making excuses for not acting when I feel a strong conviction, right?"

"Yes."

"You were wrong."

Carla laughed. "Oh, really?"

"I did that, and now I'm completely embarrassed and utterly humiliated."

"Utterly?"

"I'm baring my heart and soul, and you're picking on me?"

"I'm trying to lighten the mood. I'd ask for more details, but I'm guessing you can't tell me?"

"It's classified."

"Of course it is."

"But I felt strongly about something, and I brought it to my supervisor, who thought I was losing my mind, then I brought it to the assistant director, who—"

"Hang on, you went above your boss to *her* boss? That probably wasn't the best idea."

"What was I supposed to do? No one was listening to me."

"Are they listening now?"

"You're not making me feel any better."

"I'm your friend, but I've raised you since you were ten years old, so I'm kind of a surrogate mom too. That means I have to give it to straight when it's in your best interest."

"You *are* my mom. You're the only real one I've ever had."

"Don't say that."

"Why not? It's true."

"Sarah did the best she knew how to do."

"Don't make excuses for her," Em said as she dodged through a crowd of tourists.

"I'm not making excuses. She and I had a hard upbringing. Not everyone handles trauma the same."

"You turned out okay."

"That's because I dealt with my baggage."

"She could have too."

"It's harder for some people."

"So you *are* making excuses."

Carla sighed. "Not to change the subject or anything, but I got another postcard from your sister."

"That is changing the subject."

"She's in Phnom Penh, apparently."

"What's she doing in Cambodia?"

"Your guess is as good as mine. It says the same as the others, 'The world is so big. I wish you could see it.'"

"Charming."

"You know what I'm going to say."

"I *have* forgiven her," Em said before smiling an apology to a woman she'd bumped into. "That doesn't mean I have to be impressed that all anyone in my family cares about is themselves."

"Ouch."

"You know I don't mean you."

"Look, you've had a bump in the road, and it's made you grouchy. Tonight, we'll get all dressed up, and I'll take you to that Indonesian restaurant you love. Then I'll make weird faces at you until you can't stop laughing, okay?"

Em let her tension out in one long breath. "Thank you for still looking out for me, even though I'm a grown woman."

"We all need people in our lives who care about us."

Em glanced at a TV in the window of the shop she was walking by. "Yes we—"

"Yes we what?" Carla said. "You still there? Em? I think I lost you."

"No." She stared at the screen. "I'm here. It's just…"

"What is it?"

Em read the ticker running across the bottom of the screen as the news item continued.

"There's been an explosion," she said, her voice struggling to rise above a whisper.

"Where? Are you okay?"

"Not here. It's on the news."

"Oh. Is it bad? Does it have to do with your work?"

"I've got to go. I'll call you later." She stumbled backward, turning for the office.

"Are you going to be okay?"

"It's bad. I don't—pray, Carla. Just pray." She hung up before her aunt could ask any questions and ran as fast as she could in heels.

She'd been right, but she hadn't done enough to stop it.

Chapter 2

JEP'S LEATHER jacket rasped as he climbed from his motorcycle. He slid his helmet off and hooked it under his arm as he looked up at the workshop. The sad, drooping roof at the front, along with the small rotting sheds to either side, made it look like a frowning monkey. Not good if he was going to grow his business. And that wasn't the only thing. His lack of motivation and the guys he had working for him made for dreary prospects. He was beginning to wonder if this project had been a mistake from the beginning. Then he remembered he hadn't had much in the way of options. Maybe today was a good one to have off.

He held his helmet in both hands, about to put it back on and drive away, when a monstrous crash came from inside.

"Oh, for crying out loud." He looked up at the sky. "I can't leave them alone for five minutes?" he asked of heaven, not expecting a response. "That's great. I've

Jep

gone from stopping terrorists to babysitting. I must be the luckiest guy in the world."

At the sound of another crash, he set his helmet on the seat of the motorcycle before running inside.

At the back of the workshop, Jep found exactly what he expected. Two men fighting for probably no good reason.

"Hey!" he yelled as rushed between them, accidentally intercepting a punch that was meant for the other guy.

"Boss!" the guy who'd hit him yelled as Jep ducked away with his hand clutching his face.

"Look what you did, Moses," the second one yelled as they both went to check on him, hovering until Jep roared, throwing his arms up and pushing them both away.

"That's enough," he said, prodding his cheek bone.

"It was an accident," Moses said. He was a big guy, but clumsy and awkward, and he had the biggest, darkest eyes Jep had ever seen. "But Slate—"

"Save it." Jep righted a shelving unit that had been tipped back against the wall. "What I don't need are excuses."

"What can we do to make it right?" Slate said, picking up the bottles and tools that had fallen on the floor. He was tall, but not as tall as Moses, and gangly. A wild mane of reddish-blonde hair sat heavier on one side than the other, and the same color stubble flecked across his cheeks and chin.

"How about you two stop wrecking my shop every

time you have a disagreement?" Jep said. "Or is that too hard?"

"Why don't you tell him what you said, Slate," Moses said, squaring up to him again.

"Whoa." Jep put a hand on Moses's broad chest. At six-foot-six, he made Jep's six-two look short. But Moses got overemotional in a fight, which added to his clumsiness. It was the reason Jep had easily taken him down when they'd first met. But it was that emotion that drew him to Moses. He had a big heart. He just didn't know how to manage it.

"I didn't say anything that wasn't true," Slate said. "You were leaving streaks. I'm not the one who's terrible at my job."

"Oh-ho, you're the big man now with the boss standing between us," Moses said.

"Hey," Jep said. "I said enough. Slate, are you talking about that blue Escort?"

"Yeah," Slate said. "He's making a mess."

"No kidding," Jep said. "That's the point. You guys are learning. All of you. That's why you're here, isn't it?" He looked at both the men. "Isn't it?"

"Yes, sir," they said in unison.

"But that doesn't include wasting your paint because he's not paying enough attention," Slate mumbled.

"You let me worry about that."

"I wasn't wasting anything," Moses sulked. "And I'm sorry I hit you, Boss."

"I'm not worried about the paint or the punch. The whole point of you being here is to give you room to make mistakes so that, when you have a real customer, you do it right. And Slate, don't make me bring up your work ethic when you first started here. I almost kicked you out, remember?"

Moses snickered until Jep gave him a look. "Sorry, Boss."

"Maybe you two need to call it a day."

"No, we're cool," Slate said. "We're cool, right Moses?"

Moses stared him down. "I'm cool with Jep, not with you."

"You could try apologizing," Jep said to Slate.

Slate started fidgeting, and Moses waved a hand at him. "You know what? Forget it. I'm outta here. Jep, thank you for everything you've done. But I don't have to put up with this."

"Moses, wait," Jep said. But he didn't. "Moses." Jep caught up with him at the door and followed him out. "You're not really leaving."

"I can't stand that guy. You want me to stay? Get rid of him."

"I'm not getting rid of Slate. Take tonight to think about it. You won't find another opportunity like this, and you know it."

"Maybe it was a mistake to take you up on your offer in the first place."

"It wasn't."

"How do you know?"

"Because I know what your other options were. You really want to go back to jail?" When Moses didn't look convinced, Jep added, "You can't tell me that the guys you run with out there are easier to deal with than Slate."

"Some of them are."

"Anywhere you go, you'll meet people who are difficult. The best thing you can do is learn to deal with it without flying off the handle. Why do you think I put you on with Slate in the first place? I knew you guys would butt heads."

"You did that on purpose?"

"In life, you need to learn to work with whatever circumstances you're faced with."

"I can't work with someone who doesn't respect me."

"Of course you can. People do it all the time." He put a hand on Moses and leaned into him. "And Slate's not giving you a hard time because he disrespects you, you know. He's always afraid that the new guy is going to replace him. He grew up in and out of foster care, like you. Now he's waiting to be booted out of here. It's the first place where he's felt at home in his life. You just have to give him time."

Jep had had his own confrontations with Slate over the last year. He was way too cocky for his own good, but they had made progress. That didn't make Jep want to give up on the whole show any less. If only life had presented him with a better offer.

"Time? You want me to give him time? His problem will not be solved with time. You want me back, you get rid of him."

"You know I won't do that. You all deserve a chance."

Jep

"Not even over that fight? You want me to tell you what he really said? The exact words?"

"I don't need you to. I know him better than you do. But you're telling me you can handle a fist to the face but not some rude words?"

"I don't like him."

"I don't always like him either. Or you, for that matter. But I'd like you both to stay. Work through your trouble. It will be worth it in the end. I don't want to lose you over a few words."

Moses tsked, then shook his head, his dark eyes brightening a little. "Fine. I'll think about it."

"That's all I'm asking."

Moses waved dismissively as he trudged to his car, an old beat up Honda Accord that Jep had salvaged for him so he could get to work.

The alternator belt shrieked as Moses turned the engine over. Jep had forgotten to show him how to change it. And it was possible he'd never get the chance now.

Moses peeled out of the driveway, spewing blue-tinged smoke that mingled with the tiny stones and dust that kicked into the air as he sped off.

Jep waved uselessly, then walked toward the workshop, testing his face. It was puffy, but it hadn't been the hardest hit he'd ever taken.

Inside, Slate was cleaning up the mess he and Moses had made. He sniffed as Jep passed him. "Good riddance to him," he said, straightening the oil filters.

Jep spun and shoved him against the hood of a car,

pinning him there. He wasn't angry, but these guys didn't always listen unless you forced them to.

"That's how you want to handle this?" Jep said, pressing his forearm into Slate's sternum. "I expect better from you. You've been here the longest. You know more than anyone how you need to behave."

"But he—"

"You think I invite you guys here because you have a right to be here? You're grown men. Working in this place is a privilege. You should be able to sort out your own problems."

"Yes, sir."

He gave him one more shove before he stepped back and shook himself out. "Go home."

"But—"

"That's what you get for treating others worse than you want to be treated."

"Yes, sir."

"And Slate?"

"Yeah?" he mumbled, keeping his focus on the cracked concrete floor. He toed an oil stain.

"I'll see you back here in the morning?"

Slate's jaw flexed several times before he responded. "If that's what you want."

"It is. You're not going to get rid of me that easy. You got it? Besides, someone needs to clean up the rest of this mess, and it won't be me."

Slate nodded. "Then I'll see you in the morning." He trudged to the door, his shoulders slumped.

Jep ran his hand through his hair and looked around

him. Was this what the rest of his life would look like? He wasn't sure he would last.

He went to his office, a temporary walled-off area with a large flimsy window so he could see into the workshop.

He sat down at a bench he'd repurposed from a sawmill that he used as a desk and pulled his Bible out of the top drawer of a filing cabinet.

After flipping it open to where he'd been reading in Genesis, he knotted his fingers into his hair and glared at the verses he'd read the day before in chapter forty.

Please remember me and do me a favor when things go well for you. Mention me to Pharaoh, so he might let me out of this place. For I was kidnapped from my homeland, the land of the Hebrews, and now I'm here in prison, but I did nothing to deserve it.

Jep stared out the window but didn't see anything. He hadn't chosen this life. All he was doing was making the best of a bad situation. If his methods had been accepted at his old job, he'd still be saving the country, one terrorist at a time. But it had been about more than that. Richard Lawson, the assistant director, had never liked him. Jep had always been seen as an outcast. He'd even hear some of them make derogatory comments about his birth. Apparently, having a prostitute for a mom made you unfit to be a federal agent. They couldn't all be from top pedigrees.

But he'd never expected to be ousted. Not that anyone on the team would call it that. If he'd tried to stay, though, it would have gotten ugly. Maybe Moses was right. Maybe it was better not working in the same place as those who disrespect you. But working here wasn't much better, and after the fight between Slate and Moses, it was hard to see that any good was being done.

He looked back at the open Bible. For a long time, he'd identified with David, conquering giants. Now he felt an awful lot like Joseph being stuck in prison for a crime he didn't commit, and no one knew or cared that he existed.

Chapter 3

THE OFFICE WAS in chaos when Emery returned. Other departments had arrived to help carry the load, and the air was humming with angry adrenaline, their grief focused on destroying those who were responsible.

Geoff Pearce, a senior agent who was one of the few who hadn't been on the mission, was leaning against the wall near Emery's desk looking at his phone. She didn't know him very well, but he'd always been nice to her and answered her questions more patiently than any of the others.

"Agent Pearce?" she said.

He looked up but kept his phone in front of him.

"I know you must be very busy," she said. "I just… did we…how many did we lose?"

He pressed his lips together and walked to her desk, pulling out her chair. "Why don't you sit."

"It's that bad?"

"Please." He nodded toward the seat.

He pulled another chair around for himself.

"Did anyone make it?" she asked.

"I saw you talk to Murati quite a lot when she was in the office."

Em pressed a hand to her chest. "She's gone?"

"We've confirmed her and Nicholson so far. But we expect there to be more. I'm sorry. I know this is hard."

"I shouldn't be—I mean, there are others who were closer to them. And their families…I can't imagine."

"We have a lot of questions that need answering, and unfortunately I don't have the time right now to go through yours."

"I know. I don't want to keep you. I saw it on the news and rushed back, so I hadn't heard anything yet."

"You going to be okay?"

"Don't worry about me. You go."

He stood and patted her shoulder. Then the assistant director called him from across the room, and he was gone.

She opened her emails, scanning through what had come in. There wouldn't be a lot for her to do right now, which was helpful because it was impossible to concentrate. The others didn't have the luxury of spinning out or losing focus like she did. She was glad that her heart being in a million pieces wouldn't put any more lives at risk or disrupt the investigation. But could she have prevented their deaths? Murati had two kids and a husband who would suffer for the rest of their lives for what she couldn't stop.

She peered over her computer screen at the two agents talking nearby, listening to the details they relayed to each other until her desk phone rang, startling her.

She quickly lifted the handset. "Hi, yes, this is Em Chapman."

"Can I see you in my office?" It was Gardener.

"I'll be right there."

Her gaze lifted as she crossed the room to a large monitor on the wall playing live coverage of the explosion.

She stopped when she saw a covered body being wheeled toward an ambulance. After closing her eyes to erase the image, she continued to Gardener's office.

"You wanted to see me?" Em said when she entered the room.

"Sit down, please."

This time, when Em sat, she pressed her back into the seat. She needed the stability of the chair to keep her steady.

Gardener folded her hands on the desk. "I wanted to talk to you about what you brought me earlier."

If this was what it took for them to take notice of her, it was a high price to pay. "My concerns about the mission? Or the files?"

"Both. It raises some difficult questions."

"I'll answer you as best as I can. Whatever I can do to help."

"Good. Because the way I see it, this has gone one of two ways. Either you had information from an unknown source that you did not share with me, giving you inside knowledge—or it was simply coincidence."

"I—" Em's voice caught in her throat for a second. She cleared it. "I would never withhold information. If I had had anything else to share with you, I would have."

"So you're saying it was coincidence?"

Em bit down on the inside of her cheek in an attempt to bolster her confidence, but too much tragedy had happened for her to feel anything but pain. "I don't believe it was coincidence."

"Then what was it?"

"I had seen most of what was in the reports. I have access to most of the intel and the details of the operations. I think what happened was that everything I knew came together. I couldn't find the details in the files, but I interpreted—"

"Em, let me stop you there. You've been with the organization long enough to know that sometimes an operation goes wrong. Agents get killed. It's part of the job. This is not a profession devoid of failure or tragedy. But our role as analysts is to make sure we minimize the risk and present the information in a way that is beneficial to the team."

"Yes. I agree."

"That's why, since all you had was a bad feeling, it was nothing more than the two things colliding on the same day. I would bet money that you've had similar anxiety on past operations where you knew the risk was high. But when everything turned out okay, you forgot all about it. It's just that this time, things didn't turn out okay."

"I appreciate what you're saying, but—"

Gardener put her hand up. "If you can promise me that you had no other knowledge of today's event, and you haven't been in contact with anyone, then we're done here. But if you have spoken to someone, this is your last chance to tell me without serious ramifications. Withholding valuable intel on a crime like this would be…irresponsible to say the least. I don't think I need to remind you that lives were lost today."

"No. What happened today… I wish I could say that I did know more. I wish I could shed some light on what happened. But I can't." Em picked at her fingers. "I wish I could have done something to stop it."

"With the information we had, there was nothing any of us could have done. Now that we've cleared that up, there's no point focusing on the past."

"But if I'd—"

"I was a touch harsh during our last conversation, I know. I admit that. But my impatience is a symptom of the high expectations I have for you. I see you as my protégé of sorts. You could be the future of this task force. Then you will be the one sitting in my seat, and you'll understand better the difficulty of this position and what it takes to run this side of the department. That team out there needs us to be as sharp as we can be. We look at the data, analyze it, and bring them clarity and focus to help facilitate their side of the equation. They're the ones who have to think on their feet and go with their gut instinct in times of chaos and crisis. That's not our job, Emery. And if I can't count on you to be objective, then I can't have you in this role. It's too dangerous. Do you understand?"

"Yes, ma'am."

"Then you agree that your earlier concerns were subjective and merely coincidence in connection to the unfolding situation?"

What could she say? "Yes."

"And you believe you can rise above your feelings and sensitivities and bring a higher level of professionalism to your role?"

"Yes, ma'am."

"Then I trust this is the last time we need to speak about it. Now, we have a lot of work to do. We've lost good agents, and we have to help the others find out why. Can I count on you to do that?"

Em nodded.

"You're dismissed."

Emery left Gardener's office and went straight to the bathroom. She'd convinced herself that God had more for her to do in this role than manage information. But even if she had a gift for interpreting details and following God's leading, she'd misread the situation badly. Or maybe Gardener was right, maybe Em had let the fear get to her, and it had steered her into a position she couldn't get out of without humiliating herself.

Staring at herself in the mirror only increased her anxiety, so she splashed water on her face. None of it mattered anymore. She'd tried and failed. Her job was to sift through information and organize it. That was all. She could encourage a friend at church or let God guide her in personal matters, but from now on, it would stay out of the office if she wanted to keep a job she loved. It was a hard lesson to learn, but she'd absorb it quickly. She wanted to be fully available to do her job to the best of her ability.

After ripping a paper towel from the dispenser, she blotted her face, then risked another look in the mirror.

She was a little blotchy, but they all had more important things on their minds than her complexion, so she tugged her blouse to straighten it and headed back to her desk.

The bullpen was quiet when she returned. There were a few murmurs, but everyone's attention was directed to where Assistant Director Lawson was standing beside the deputy director.

Lawson stepped forward. "Thank you for your attention. I'm sorry to interrupt when you're so busy with important matters, but Deputy Director Truman would like to say a few words."

There had been an ongoing feud between Truman and Lawson but only speculation as to what it stemmed from. This was the first time since Emery had started working with the task force that Truman had visited them.

"Thank you," Truman said before clearing his throat. "I know your time is valuable, so I will keep this short. I would first like to offer you my sincere condolences, as I know you've lost not just colleagues but friends. The agency is poorer for it. But I'd like you all to know that finding who is responsible and how it happened in the first place is our first priority. We are putting our full weight behind this. I thank you all for your hard work, and I know you will all do everything in your power to uncover the answers we need. In saying that, however, as of the end of the week, we will be disbanding this task force."

Murmurs rose, and Emery's heart sank, but it was

Lawson who drew the most attention by the shocked look on his face. It was news to him.

Truman continued. "You will be given your new assignments over the next several days, and, unfortunately, that means some of you will be unable to continue with this investigation. However, we will endeavor to keep you in the loop until it is resolved."

"Sir," Lawson said. His face had turned reddish-purple, but he kept his voice even. "Can we have a word?"

Truman kept his focus on the crowd. "This shouldn't come as a surprise for anyone here, and I would expect it to be a welcome change for most of you. You are now severely short-staffed, and over the past couple of years, your completion rates have fallen dramatically."

"That's because the group we're up against is employing new tactics," Lawson said. "We've been working nearly blindfolded. Operating on limited intel. From where I'm sitting, we're doing well with what we have. We're the best unit to continue this investigation."

"I'm sorry to—" Truman tried to interject, but Lawson wouldn't let him.

"We were always an experiment. One of our core goals was trying out new strategies. Looking for chinks in the armor of our enemy. We were given discretion because of that."

Truman shook his head. "It was an experiment that worked at one time. It doesn't anymore. I'm sorry to bring this to you all on such short notice, but making the changes now will mean less disruption into the future. I don't make this decision lightly."

Jep

"All we need is more time," Lawson said. "We're getting close. We've been successful in the past; we can be successful again."

"You've had time. So unless you have a magic formula to turn back the clock, I'm afraid we're finished here."

"If I may." Agent Pearce stepped forward. "Perhaps there is a way to go back in time and see if we can't bring back the success we had."

"What exactly do you mean?" Truman said.

"We're short agents right now, but several years ago, when this task force was at peak performance, we had one who was excellent. A real standout. He did the job of four men at least."

Lawson scowled at Pearce, trying to stop him from continuing.

Em looked between the two men, wondering what was happening. She didn't have to wait long.

"Who's this agent?" Truman said.

Pearce glanced at Lawson briefly before he said, "Jep Booth."

Lawson shook his head. "Out of the question."

"Wasn't he fired?" Truman said.

Pearce looked at Lawson again. "Not exactly."

"He should have been," Lawson said. "For all the trouble he caused. He's as good as fired. We can't bring him back. It's too late. He was asked to leave. Lucky for us, he complied."

"So he wasn't fired?" Truman said.

"His methods were unconventional," Pearce said.

"And he didn't fit in, but he was better than anyone at his job."

"This task force was successful despite Booth," Lawson said. "Not because of him."

"He had the contacts, and he was always two steps ahead," Pearce said, turning his attention to Lawson. "I know you didn't like him, sir, but you have to admit, he was very good."

"*Like* had nothing to do with it," Lawson said. "This isn't a playground. Jep posed a threat."

"Not enough of a threat to fire him," Truman said with a nod. "That's what we need right now, because that's what the enemy has been doing to us. I remember him. Only met him a few times, but he was exceptional. He got the job done. All right. I'll give you a reprieve. I'll delay shutting you down and give you time to see if you can bring in Jep and turn things around."

"But—" Lawson said.

"Unless you can offer me a better solution?" He lifted his eyebrows, waiting.

"I'd prefer if we talked about this in my office."

"From what I can see, there's nothing to discuss. I've made my decision."

"He doesn't have the agency's best interest in mind. He never has."

"Does he have America's best interest in mind? Because that's all we need right now. Once we catch the terrorists and bring them to justice, we can reevaluate."

"I still object."

"Nevertheless, I want you to do whatever it takes to bring him back. This group is on its last legs. You've all

Jep

done your duty, but we need better. Jep Booth is your last chance. Good luck. Keep me updated on your progress."

Lawson waited until Truman left before turning on Pearce and dragging him aside. They were close enough to Em's desk that she could hear them despite their lowered voices.

"What were you thinking?" Lawson said.

"I know you never liked Jep, but Truman was going to shut us down. Would you rather that?"

"Jep's a bomb waiting to go off."

"I'd say time has tempered him."

"You weren't here long enough to know how he was."

"Would you rather we all get transferred?" Pearce said.

"I can't believe Truman did that to me."

"He didn't give you any indication before coming here?"

"He's been threatening me for a year to shut us down. I thought it was all for show. He knew I wouldn't say much with my entire team watching."

"At least we have a stay of execution."

"You had better hope Jep steps up to the task."

"We should move on this now," Pearce said.

"Fine. If you want him so bad, you go get him."

"Me? I didn't know him well. I think he'd be more convinced if you showed up."

Lawson chuckled darkly. "You think so? You think he's going to throw a welcoming party when the feds turn up at his door led by me? No. You're going. It's better he meets with someone he doesn't have a tainted history with. But I don't want to get any complaints when he breaks your nose." Lawson turned and noticed Emery. "On second thought, bring her."

"Emery?" Pearce said.

"He probably won't hit you with a pretty face to distract him."

Emery hid her blanch well, but she wouldn't object, not with so much riding on this guy Jep coming back on the team. If her presence encouraged this guy to be more agreeable, then she'd do her part. But beyond the initial visit, she would steer clear. The last thing she needed was more trouble.

"You really think that's necessary?" Pearce said.

"I'm not saying she has to go on a date with the guy, but if we're going to get him back through those doors—" Lawson jammed his finger toward the elevator. "We need to use what resources we have. Do you have any problem with that, Miss Chapman?"

"Uh, all you need me to do is be present?"

"You think you can do that?"

"Yeah. I'm okay with that."

"Good. Pearce, you let me know if you hit any snags."

"Yes, sir."

Chapter 4

"I KNOW you're not happy about this," Pearce said to Em, who was staring out the window at the tree line.

"I'm an analyst," she said. "This wasn't in the job description, but we all have to be willing to do what we can."

"I was disappointed in Lawson when he suggested it, but he's right. Jep is an unknown quantity for us right now. Think of it as a mission if it helps. When we put our teams together, we choose from the strengths we know we have. Right now, we need someone who can have a calming effect on the scenario. But don't worry. I won't let anything happen to you."

"Do you expect to *need* to protect me from this guy?"

"There's no reason to think so."

"That's not very comforting."

Pearce laughed. "I have been in this task force for a couple years now, and comforting is not something I've ever tried to be."

"Not in your job description?" She grinned. "But what about you?"

"Me?"

"Yeah. What if he *does* go for you?"

"I can handle myself, but I doubt he'd try anything. He and Lawson obviously don't like each other much, but he doesn't have any reason not to like me. We didn't cross paths much. He left not long after I turned up."

"Can you remember if he got along with anyone?"

"It was all or nothing with that guy. You either loved him or hated him."

"So, not everyone wanted him gone?"

"Some of us respected that he got the job done, even if we didn't agree with his methods. But mostly he rubbed people the wrong way. "

"Especially Lawson."

"Exactly."

"Are you allowed to tell me what he did that got him…removed?"

"It was a lot of things. He wasn't great at following orders. He dressed differently from everyone else. He said whatever was on his mind. And that's just what I saw."

"There had to be more. Lawson wouldn't hate him for that."

"There was something between them, but you'll have to ask them."

"He obviously likes women." Em squirmed in her seat. "Otherwise I wouldn't be here as window dressing."

Jep

Pearce grimaced. "How about if you stay in the car?"

"No. I can handle it. I'm here. I may as well let him see me."

"Don't worry, he'll see you. The first thing he'll do is check who else I brought with me. He'll be curious at the very least."

"And what happens if he agrees to return?"

"I'll try to get him to come back to the office right away. There are formalities we'll need to address to reinstate him. But you won't have to do anything else. Once we get back to the office, you can retreat to your desk and get back to work."

They pulled onto a dirt driveway that opened up into a wide parking lot with broken-down cars littering the yard. Pearce parked toward the back of the lot.

"This is the place?" Em said when Pearce turned off the car. "It's a dump."

"It could use a little spruce up."

She looked at him. "If you're not careful, that roof could cave in on you. You were hoping he'd be better with time, but I'd say there's a good chance he's let himself go. We've profiled guys like this. The kind who don't work well with authority and don't like following the rules. I'd say he held a grudge when he left, and he's waiting for an opportunity to blow a fuse."

"It will be okay. I'll feel him out. If I don't think he's cut out to come back, we'll leave him here."

"And then what?"

"Then my idea blows up in my face, and we have

the drive back to the office to come up with another plan."

"Another plan that Truman will go for."

"Let's hope the outside of this place doesn't reflect what's inside."

She said, "Good luck" as Pearce got out of the car, but silently, she was praying.

God, all I ask is that this works out Your way. If this task force is meant to continue, then I pray Mr. Booth is agreeable. If not, give Pearce wisdom. Give us all wisdom.

She chewed on her nail as Pearce walked toward the building. She wavered between hoping Jep was crazy and hoping he wasn't. Thankfully, she wasn't the one who had to make the decision. She would sacrifice her comfort if Jep could really be an asset to the team, but she'd be one of the lucky few who wouldn't need to have much interaction with him.

And don't let this end in a fight. I don't want Pearce to get hurt. If Jep didn't play by the rules and he was mentally unstable, it was impossible to guess what might happen.

Jep ran his hand along the front fender of a black Camaro.

"Not bad," he said.

"Not bad?" Slate slammed his hands onto his hips. "That's as good as the Mona Lisa."

"You plan on hanging it in a museum?"

"You know what I mean."

Jep grinned. "It is good. You've got a talent for this.

And you're getting the work done in good time. Your future customers are going to love that."

"You bet they will."

"But can I give you a tip?"

"Sure."

"Customers don't like cocky."

"It's called confidence."

"You want to know the difference between cocky and confident?"

"Not really."

"Too bad. I'm going to tell you anyway."

Slate rolled his eyes. "Here we go."

"Confidence can keep to itself. Cocky has to make sure everyone knows."

"Yeah, yeah, yeah."

"I'm serious."

"I know. I got it. You don't want me to show off."

"Let your work speak for itself, because I can tell you right now. It does."

"Thank you."

"You're welcome." Jep continued around the car, looking for defects.

"So...," Slate began, tucking his hands into the pockets of his overalls. "I was thinking."

"Oh, yeah?"

"Yeah. Moses was telling me how he'd had a job fitting car stereos."

"On cars he'd stolen?"

"You're the one who taught me not to ask questions I don't want the answers to."

"Ah, so you *are listening*."

"I always listen. Anyway, I thought maybe we could diversify."

"Moses hasn't come back."

"He will."

Jep kept a rein on his grin. If he looked too pleased, Slate would clam up. "How do you know that?"

"I talked to him."

"Oh, yeah?"

"Yeah. He's visiting his sister, then he said he'd be back."

"He hasn't spoken to me about this."

"I told him I'd let you know."

Jep nodded slowly. "It's nice to know you guys are finding a way to get along."

"Yeah, well…" He cleared his throat. "I feel bad about your black eye. It's kind of my fault. I'm not proud of what I said to Moses…so…I apologized."

"Did it hurt?"

"It's about the worst thing ever. But *you* don't have any trouble saying it, so I thought I'd give it a shot."

"It gets easier."

"What would be easier is not having to apologize in the first place."

"Being perfect is a whole lot harder than being humble." He rested a hand on Slate's shoulder. "I'm proud of you."

Slate shrugged it off. "It's nothin'."

"Hey, Boss." A thirteen-year-old kid with a buzz cut ran inside, his two-sizes-too-big Nikes thumping across the floor as he came. "There's some dude in a suit outside."

"A suit?" Slate said. "I thought Jep told you to stop drinking or you couldn't hang around anymore."

"I'm not drinking. Go see for yourself." His voice cracked at the end.

"Did he give you a name?" Jep said.

"Yeah." The kid leaned in and lowered his voice. "Called himself Agent Geoffrey Pearce."

Slate balked. "Agent? What, you mean like a travel agent?"

Jep's cheek twitched. "Not that kind of agent. You're sure he said his name was Pearce?"

"Yeah, he made me repeat it back ta him like he's some important dude and I'm an idiot. It's probably a scam. That's what my gramma says. Everyone's tryin' ta scam everybody these days."

"I'll go talk to him," Jep said. He could remember the name but not the face.

His nonchalant walk through to the main workshop and then to the front of the building hid the fact that this news had him wound up tight.

He wiped his hands on the rag he was carrying when he spotted Pearce, and the face came back. They hadn't had much to do with each other in the short time they'd both worked on the task force. He would prefer going into this conversation knowing why the agent was here, but he couldn't even begin to guess.

"Agent Pearce," he said, almost looking his visitor up and down in an act of intimidation, but he held back. He'd only appear aggressive if necessary. Lawson had been good to his word about leaving him alone. Until now. Jep would hide his strength in case he needed it as a surprise. "This is unexpected."

"It's good to see you again, Mr. Booth."

"Call me Jep."

"Jep. I would have called, but I didn't know your number."

Jep shook Pearce's offered hand, then stepped back and looked at the car. "Don't know my number, just my address?" Someone was in the passenger seat, but the interior was too dark to see who it was.

"How've you been?" Pearce pointed toward his face. "You get in a fight?"

"I got in the middle of one."

Pearce looked around the overgrown block. "Nice place you've got here."

"No, it's not. Why are you here?"

"I remember you always being straight to the point."

"Do you?"

"I'm not here looking for a fight."

"That's good."

"My visit is...I was going to say positive, but the circumstances aren't the best. There's been an incident."

"An incident?"

"Yes."

Jep narrowed his eyes. "That wouldn't happen to be related to the gas leak that leveled a city block last week?" He laughed when Pearce flinched. "You can keep the media in the dark, but anyone with half a brain can read between the lines. Did you lose anyone?" The smile slid off his face at Pearce's frown.

Jep

"We lost four," Pearce said. "Two more are in the hospital. We think they'll make it."

"Who'd you lose?"

"Nicholson, Gonzalez, Murati, and Gill."

He knew Murati and Gill. Gill had been a good friend. "Did you come here to give your condolences?"

"No." Pearce paused. "I came to ask for your help."

"You looking for someone to pin this on?"

"Of course not."

"There is no way you came here to get my help for the agency." Jep took a step closer. "Tell me why you're really here."

Pearce didn't back down as Jep moved in. "We both know you didn't do yourself any favors while you were an agent."

"I did my job."

Jep's eyes shifted when he saw the car door open, but he was surprised to see a blonde get out. She was fair-skinned and delicate looking. Her silk blouse pressed against her body in the breeze as she stepped from behind the door. She was a strange figure here amongst the tall weeds and rusted metal. A flower growing in the middle of a junkyard. An odd choice to bring for backup.

"Who's that?" he asked.

"Emery Chapman."

"Not *Agent* Chapman?"

"She's an analyst."

"Why is she here?" When Pearce didn't answer, Jep chuckled. "I get it. Now it all makes sense."

"What does?"

"She's pretty. I can see why you chose her."

"She happens to be an excellent analyst."

"But that's not why she's here. Does *she* know why you brought her? To soften the blow? You expected me to erupt? I should after the way I was treated."

"I'm not here to fight with you."

"I hope not. I'd hate for her to see you covered in blood. Has she ever seen blood before? My guess is no."

Pearce's hand moved to his gun and rested there. "I don't want things to get ugly, but I'll do what I have to if you're going to get aggressive."

"Isn't that what you were expecting? That's why she's here."

Pearce looked at Emery and waved her back into the car.

Her lips pursed. She didn't like being dismissed. Jep was disappointed when she obeyed. The type of worker bee who always did what they were told. That was everyone's problem with him. He was the exact opposite.

"Is this her first time in the field?" Jep said. "She would have been better off staying back at the office with the cozy blue carpet. Is it still blue? I liked that carpet. Not always practical, but it felt nice. Intimate."

"Maybe this was a mistake."

"Most likely."

Pearce sighed and dropped his hand away from his gun. "The problem is, I don't have many options."

"Options for what?"

Jep

"The task force. We're in a difficult situation, and we'd like you to consider coming back."

Jep struggled to make sense of what Pearce had said. "Is this a joke? You came all this way to make a joke?"

"I'm not kidding. We need you."

Jep ran his hand over his head and rubbed it hard. Pearce had been right to bring Emery Chapman with him, but not for the reason she was there. Her presence was so outlandish Pearce had to be telling the truth.

"What do you think?" Pearce said when Jep couldn't find a fitting response.

"Whose idea was it? Because I know for certain it wasn't the assistant director's."

"Actually, it was mine. Truman wants to shut down the task force."

"What does that have to do with me?"

"You're the leverage to keep it going. We bring you in, and Truman gives us more time."

"Truman wants me back? Man, you guys must be in trouble."

"I was around long enough to know you did your job very well. I thought maybe you could do that again."

"What does Lawson have to say about it?"

"He's the one who sent me to get you."

"But Lawson doesn't want me?"

"He has agreed. I told you, he sent—"

"I'm going to have to hear it from his own mouth."

"If you come back, you'll see him at the office."

Jep had strong reasons that tugged him firmly one way, then the other. It wasn't the workshop he was worried about. He had a friend who could come in and look after the shop and the boys while he was away. But as much as it had felt like a prison, he knew where he stood with these boys. If he returned with Pearce, he'd be entering unknown and probably hostile territory.

Chapter 5

EMERY FOLDED her hands in her lap. When Jep had come out to meet Pearce, he had been exactly what she'd expected. He was solemn and dark and had a black eye that suggested he was a man accustomed to fighting. But he'd also looked unimpressed, bored even. That was until he'd closed in on Pearce.

His black T-shirt, although basic, made for an imposing figure. She'd seen Pearce in training and knew he could handle himself, but in his suit, he looked less the threat than Jep Booth, whose biceps stretched his sleeves when he crossed his arms. That was when she'd thought it was time to show herself, only to be dismissed again. She had a lot of work to do. Sitting in the car wasn't helping anyone.

She listened to snippets of their conversation through her opened window, but she didn't catch enough to know what was going on or whether their conversation had taken a more positive turn.

Then Jep sidestepped Pearce and headed her way.

She straightened, then tugged at her skirt and pushed back in the seat right before he arrived at her window.

"Hi there, Em," Jep said, resting his forearm in the window frame.

She shifted away, but his scent followed her. A mix of mint and what reminded her of pine needles. "It's Emery."

"Right. Emery. I have a quick question for you."

Her heart raged in her chest. She hadn't been briefed for this scenario. When her eyes darted to Pearce, Jep shifted to block her view.

"Don't worry about him. I'm the one you need to focus on. When the assistant director, Richard Lawson, was told I would be asked back on the team, what did he say?"

She lifted her chin. "I don't remember."

"Course you do. I can see it on your face. What'd he say?"

She wasn't about to let him decide what she did or didn't remember, no matter what her face betrayed. "I honestly don't. But after what I heard about your behavior while you were on the team, you can't expect he would be excited about the prospect of your return."

Every part of her body throbbed in time with her pulse. She wasn't normally so forward, but if Jep was going to join them, he needed to know where she stood. His overbearing nature toward her reinforced that notion.

Unfortunately, she must have failed in her show of strength because he smiled like he was amused by her response.

Jep

"I'll tell you what," Jep said, turning his attention to Pearce. "I'll consider your proposal if you get Lawson on the phone so I can hear from his own lips that he wants me back."

Em glanced up at Pearce, who kept his face devoid of any emotional response to Jep's request.

"You won't take my word for it?" Pearce said.

"I'd prefer to know where I stand before I turn up to work. I also have a few demands that you don't have the authority to approve."

Pearce made eye contact with Em, then pulled out his phone. "Be polite if you can. Don't forget, the whole agency is going through a tough time."

"Don't worry, I *do* know how to be considerate and courteous." He smiled down at Em. "I know that's not easy for everyone."

She looked away. Having him at the office was going to be a nightmare. At least she didn't have a reason to work directly with any of the agents. All she had to do was survive this encounter. Then she'd be in the clear.

"Assistant Director?" Pearce said into the phone. "I'm here with Mr. Booth. He'd like to speak to you." He listened for a second, then handed the phone over.

Jep put the phone on speaker. "Richard Lawson, it's been a long time. How've you been?"

"You're on speaker," Pearce called out in warning.

"I hear you're interested in having me return to the team," Jep said. "Is this correct?"

"I'd say it's nice to hear your voice," Lawson said, "but we both know I'd be lying."

"I always did appreciate your candor."

"You sure about that?"

"Why don't we dismiss with the pleasantries? I know you're very busy right now."

"Pearce will have told you the nature of our situation?" Lawson said. "Desperate times and all that."

"They were good people you lost."

"We haven't agreed on much over the years, but on that we certainly do. Which is why I hope and expect that you will take this offer with the utmost care and consideration. If you're looking to settle scores, now is not the time."

"If I agree to come back, my sole purpose will be to find whoever is responsible."

"I'm glad to hear it."

"I do have a couple of conditions, however."

Lawson's sigh was loud. "I don't believe you're in a position to require anything of us."

"No? I seem to recall that, a few minutes ago, Pearce turned up at my door to inform me that you require my services. You either need my help or you don't."

"Fine. I'll hear you out, but I'm not making any promises. What are your conditions?"

"The first one is, I get to choose my partner."

"That shouldn't be a problem. We have a group of highly skilled and effective agents on the team. I'd be happy for you to work with any one of them."

"Great. The other condition is that I have full control over any ops that we carry out."

"That's out of the question, and you know it."

"You won't even consider it?"

"No."

"Okay then. Best of luck to you all."

He held the phone out for Pearce to take when Lawson said, "Wait. I had hoped I could appeal to your sense of duty to those we lost, but I can see now you're still the same old Jep."

"I guess some things never change."

Em turned her face away so he wouldn't see the disdain. She was curious to find out Pearce's take on all of this. He wasn't giving anything away, and she had to commend him on his patience.

"I will give you control of any operations you are leading," Lawson said. "But I retain ultimate authority."

"That won't work for me. I'm sure you know why."

"That was years ago."

"You're saying you wouldn't do the same again if given the option?"

"I stand by that call."

"Even though it was wrong?"

"You disobeyed a direct order, and lives were lost."

Em glanced at Pearce, who remained blank-faced. If he'd known about whatever mission Jep was referring to, he hid it well. But she still had the files on her desk that she needed to return to the archives. She'd do a little more digging on her own and find out what happened.

"That's where you stand?" Jep said.

The line was silent for a moment, then Lawson said. "Fine. You have complete control over the ops that you are directly leading."

"Great. Then I guess I'll see you back at the office."

Em thought she noticed a wince on Jep's face when he hung up, but then he smiled smugly as he tossed the phone back to Pearce. "I guess we'll be working together."

Em waited for him to add a smart quip to her as well, but he didn't.

"Thank you," Pearce said. "I know your relationship with Lawson is strained, but we all appreciate your help. Even Lawson."

"We'll see how that manifests itself once I'm back on the team."

"We're all focused on the same goal."

"That's the idea," Jep said. "When do you want me to start?"

"The sooner the better. We'll need you to come in and get the paperwork in order before we can fill you in on all the details."

"I can take the afternoon off if you want me to come in now. The boys don't need me here for the rest of the day."

"Now would be great."

"I'll get my bike and follow you in."

"Actually, it would be better if you came in with us."

"In the car?"

"Security reasons," Pearce said. "It will be simpler that way. You understand."

"Not really. Someone will have to drive me home again."

"That won't be a problem. But you don't have clearance right now. It would be a lot of messing around."

"If you say so. I'll get my stuff and be right out."

"You're not getting changed?"

Jep

He looked down at his greasy jeans. "Good point. Give me a minute."

Pearce waited until Jep had gone back inside before he got back in the car.

"You did good," he said to Em.

"I wasn't too harsh?"

"No, I was impressed. I don't think I've heard that sort of confidence come out of you before."

"I haven't had the need. What if he asks you to be his partner?"

"I wouldn't have any problem with that."

"Really? You have way more patience than me. I spoke to him for two minutes, and I already can't stand him."

"All you have to do is ignore his arrogance and remember what a good agent he is."

"I don't have any personal experience with him as an agent, remember?"

"Then take my word for it."

"You're assuming he's on top of his game."

"He handled himself pretty well just now." He laughed at her scowl. "I told you people either love him or hate him. You're obviously the latter, but it's what makes him good at his job."

"I trust your judgement, but I don't have to like it."

"I'm sorry you had to be here for this."

"Don't be. It was good for me. It's easy to become consumed by your work when you're sitting in front of a computer all day."

Jep came outside but turned to speak to someone they couldn't see and laughed.

"This is going to be a long car ride home," Em said.

"You don't have to speak to him if you don't want to."

"Why didn't you let him come in on his bike?"

"I want to feel him out. Make sure he's right for the job."

"I thought this deal was done."

"No deal is ever final. I'm glad he's agreed to work with us, but there's no telling how things will go. We need to make sure we're on top of this."

"If there's anything I can do to help, let me know."

"You've already done more than your fair share. You don't see Gardener out here, do you?"

"I think she would have relished the opportunity to give Jep a piece of her mind."

"You're probably right."

"I'm serious, though. I don't know what I could do, but if you need me to dig back into his old cases or anything, I'm your girl."

"I'll keep that in mind. Thank you for offering."

Jep headed their way, and they went silent as he opened the door to the back seat and tossed his jacket inside before sliding in and moving to the center.

"Everyone good?" he said, leaning forward.

"We're ready if you are."

He patted Pearce's shoulder, then leaned back and put on his seatbelt with a wide grin across his face.

Em looked out her window and took a long silent breath. One more hour, and this would all be over.

Chapter 6

JEP'S FINGERS tapped on the seat beside him. He knew it wouldn't all be this easy, but so far, he'd found a lot of amusement in the two sitting in the front. Like the way Emery tried not to look at him when he got in the car.

"You're awful quiet up there, Emery," he said to see how she'd react.

"I don't speak when I have nothing to say."

"Do you have any suits in your wardrobe anymore?" Pearce said.

"I barely wore a suit when I was there before."

Emery's head turned, but she didn't look at him directly. Judging by her dress code, it must rub her the wrong way that he still wore jeans and a T-shirt with no intention of changing. He wasn't against wearing a suit, but it was easier to get information from people when you didn't look like you were above them.

"I thought I remembered that," Pearce said. "But it's worth having one or two for those occasions when you really need them."

"I remember how to do my job. Don't worry."

"Sorry, I don't mean to sound condescending."

"That's okay. You're nervous about me coming back. Afraid you've made a grave mistake."

"That's not true."

"I remember the day you started with the task force," Jep said.

"Oh, yeah?"

"You came in full of confidence and swagger. But it didn't take you long to settle into your place."

"I can't tell if you're saying that to be rude or if you mean it as a compliment."

"Compliment. I don't like it when guys are full of themselves. We didn't know each other well, but I thought you were a good addition to the team."

"I wanted to be there, so I did what I had to do to get along with everyone. I was proud to be a part of the team. I thought you were too."

"I was. We did a lot of good work."

"But you weren't willing to adjust?"

Jep huffed a laugh and looked out the window. "A word of advice—don't believe everything everyone said about me after I left."

"I came to ask for you back, didn't I?"

"That doesn't mean you haven't already made up your mind about me. I know she has."

Pearce looked at him in the rearview mirror, then looked at Emery. "Give her a good reason to think otherwise, and you'll find her a great asset to the team."

"At least I'll always know where she's at. I can appreciate that already."

Jep

He hadn't fully considered the prejudices he'd have to face back at the office. His current behavior wasn't helping opinions inside the car, but it was the protective mechanism he sometimes fell back on. If people were going to have the wrong opinion of him, it was easier to give it to them. He knew God expected better from him, so he decided to keep his mouth shut for the rest of the drive.

They rode in silence for a while until Jep noticed Emery's body go rigid. He leaned sideways so he could see out her window and follow her line of sight through to the park they were passing.

"Stop the car," he said, unbuckling his seatbelt.

"What?" Pearce said.

"Stop the car."

"Why?"

"Just do it." He slid to the passenger side and gripped the door handle.

"Jep, we have an awful lot of work to do."

"I don't care. Stop it or I'll jump." He pulled the lever far enough the door released, but he still held it closed.

Pearce took his foot off the accelerator but only slowed when they approached a red light.

"There's no time," Jep said and opened the door while the car was still moving.

"What are you doing?" Pearce said, slamming on the brake.

Jep jumped to the curb and ran into the park where a fight had already broken out. A kid in his early teens was being thrown to the ground by a couple of guys in their twenties. One of them was about to stomp on the kid, but Jep pounced, knocking him to the ground, then rolled when the second man attacked. He grabbed the guy's foot and twisted, yanking him around so he fell to the ground.

The first guy scramble across the grass and took a loose swing but missed. Jep saw the kid making a run for it, so he struck hard, knocking the first guy out before facing the second, who was on his feet with his arms in a boxing pose until he saw Pearce and Emery running toward them; then he took off at a run.

"Pearce," Jep shouted. "You get him. I'll get the boy."

He sprinted toward the kid, who'd slowed until he turned and saw Jep was after him.

Jep dropped his head and picked up speed, launching to catch the kid's legs, and they both tumbled to the ground.

The boy scratched along the ground to regain his footing, but Jep took hold of his backpack and yanked him backward.

"What'd you run for?" Jep said, out of breath.

The boy shook his head as he pushed up to sitting.

"You okay?" Jep said. "They didn't hurt you too bad?"

The boy touched his mouth where it was bloody and winced. "I'm fine, but I'd be better if you let me go. I didn't do anything."

"You want to tell me what happened back there?"

"Those guys attacked me for no reason at all."

"Then you should press charges."

"I don't want to. Can I go?"

"Maybe. What's in the bag?"

"None of your business."

"Is it drugs?"

"No."

"No meaning yes."

"It's private property. Cops can't search without a warrant."

"They can if they have probable cause."

The boy sneered. "You don't. I was the one being attacked."

"Then it's a good thing I'm not a cop. What's your name?"

"None of your business."

"Then I'll call you squirt."

"It's Bryce."

"Okay, Bryce, let's go."

"I'm not going anywhere with you."

Jep dragged him to his feet.

"Let me go!" Bryce tried to take a swing at him, but Jep caught his arm, yanking it around his back to keep him from causing any more trouble. "You're gonna break my arm," Bryce hollered.

"Then stop squirming and move."

He used the boy's trapped arm to compel him back to Em and Pearce, who were waiting for him. Pearce had caught the other guy, and they were now both sitting on the grass, restrained.

"Have you called the cops?" Jep asked Pearce as he bumped his knee into the back of Bryce's knee so he dropped to the ground.

"Do you have to be so rough?" Em said. "He's just a kid."

"Yeah," Bryce said. "I'm a kid. You should let me go."

"And aren't you two kind of like the cops?" Em asked.

"This is outside our jurisdiction," Jep said, looking inside the boy's backpack and pulling out a bag of pills.

"That's Advil," Bryce said.

"Oh, yeah? You get a lot of headaches?"

"Yeah. I do."

"Uh-huh."

Jep tried to pull the bag off his back, but Bryce crossed his arms, so Jep pulled a knife from his pocket and cut the straps.

"Hey, you can't destroy my property," Bryce said.

"Probably not. You can let the cops know you want to file a complaint when they come pick you up." He handed the bag to Pearce, who was making the call.

He sidled up beside Em, forcing her to take a step to the side. "You really don't like me," he said.

"I barely know you. But while I may not agree with your methods, you did a good job here all in all."

"Thanks."

"The police are on their way," Pearce said.

Jep pulled a card from his wallet and handed it to Bryce. "Once they let you out of Juvie or wherever you end up, call this number if you decide you'd like to a chance at a better life."

"What's this?" Bryce said.

"A once in a lifetime opportunity."

Jep

Bryce ripped the card in two and dropped it on the ground. Jep shrugged, hoping when he turned his back the boy would change his mind.

"Suit yourself," he said, then turned away and locked eyes with Emery, who had been watching the exchange. She looked away immediately.

There was more to this woman than what appeared on the surface, but it was hard to say if he'd ever find out more. Or whether the team he was about to meet would give him the benefit of the doubt. But he prepared for an icy welcome.

Once the police arrived, they were back on the road.

"That was a good pick up back there," Pearce said to him.

"It was," Emery said. "I kind of felt bad for that kid. I'm glad we were in the right place at the right time, and you were paying enough attention to do something about it."

Jep was about to tell her it was her that noticed first but decided he'd save that information for another time. Did she really not know?

It wasn't long before they were passing through the gate at headquarters, and Pearce escorted him to get his badge sorted out while Emery excused herself. She said she had to get back to work, but despite her nice comment about his work in the park, she remained prickly around him and disappeared as soon as she could.

"I should have mentioned this earlier."

"Here we go," Jep said.

"You'd already know this job is temporary at this point."

Jep blinked when the camera flashed. "I know how these things work—did that picture take okay? Or do I need to do another one?"

The camera operator showed him the picture. "You happy with that?"

He looked irritated in the photo. "That'll do. Where to next, Pearce?"

"I'll show you to your desk." He led the way to the elevator. "You already know there are some here who aren't fond of your return?"

"Besides Lawson, you mean?"

"Yes."

"I'm aware. Although I wonder how many of those people actually know me. Based on Emery's reaction, I'd say I'm going into enemy territory."

"Truman and Lawson have both approved your return, and we all want the same outcome, so I don't expect any trouble. But if you feel like you're getting ganged up on, you can come to me. I'll do what I can to support you."

"I think I can handle it. As long as you all know I won't compromise myself to make everyone else comfortable. I'll do everything in my power to get these guys, but I won't be stuffed into a box. There's no point in me coming back if everyone expects me to toe the line."

"I'm not sure how to respond to that."

"You know they never fired me, right? I left."

"Because they asked you to."

"It was mutual. I didn't do anything wrong. And I'll continue along those lines because that's what gets the job done."

"I can work with that."

"Then we should get along just fine. If there are any files I can take home with me, I'll study up. Do you have any leads so far?"

"It's been a strange one." He ushered Jep out of the elevator. Most people kept working, but a few stopped and looked. "Normally there's chatter."

"Yeah. Someone's always listening. FBI, CIA, MI6. I know the drill."

"Then you'll understand how odd it is when we have an attack or attempted attack of some kind with no forewarning at all."

"Nothing?"

"No. And this has happened over and over again."

"But you can confirm it's terrorism?"

"There have been small groups from Malaysia, Afghanistan, Yemen, Somalia, you name it, who have taken credit for various attacks."

"It's not unusual for a group that's not responsible to say they did it."

"We haven't been able to confirm or deny anything except that we're confident they're connected."

"What about this latest one?"

"The intel we got was credible, but it was still unusual. Not through the normal channels. One was a letter that was found left at an abandoned site where a suspected terrorist group was meeting. Another was at a successful operation. We didn't lose anyone, but we found more intel. I'll give you the file to read through."

"But your intel was bad."

"Everything about it suggested—"

"Good lord," Lawson said as he approached. "What happened to your face? Was that from your scuffle in the park today?"

"Lawson." Jep held out his hand, and his superior reluctantly shook. "No, this was from a previous altercation."

"You have a lot of those?"

"Not if I can help it."

Lawson sighed and finished giving Jep a once over. "I shouldn't be surprised. You haven't changed much."

"Neither have you." Both men left a lot unsaid. Each of them had nukes they could blast at the other, so there remained an unsteady truce.

Jep had been sure he'd forgiven Lawson, but the clenching anger in his gut made it clear he hadn't.

Is this why you brought me here? he prayed. *To prove a point?* That meant he'd have to find a way to let it go. Maybe if they could work together peacefully toward the same end, he'd find it easier.

"I take it everything's in order?" Lawson asked Pearce.

"Yes, sir. I've been briefing Jep on events up till now."

"Good. Jep, that desk over there can be yours. Make yourself at home."

Jep looked, his gaze sliding past his own desk to

Jep

Emery's further along. She was focused on her computer. Maybe a little too focused.

"I'll leave you two to debrief," Lawson said and made his exit.

As they crossed the room, Jep made eye contact with those who looked his way. Some smiled. Some didn't. He nodded toward Emery when she looked at him. She smiled with her lips firmly together.

"Nice," Jep said as he sat, testing out his chair. "These are new. Stiffer than the last ones but in a good way. And less squeaky."

"I don't expect you'll spend much time here."

"Hopefully not." He leaned back. "If I'm trying to look at the bright side, one good thing about being despised by your co-workers—"

"No one here despises you."

"Can you say that and look me in the eye? All I'm saying is, I have a newfound appreciation for all the trouble the boys back at the workshop gave me. Their antagonism is no match for the hostility in this room right now."

"I doubt anyone in here will give you a black eye."

"This wasn't meant for me."

Pearce smirked. "Whatever you say."

An agent he recognized from his time there before headed toward his desk.

"Agent Bailey," Jep said. "Good to see you."

"I never thought I'd see you back here again." Bailey roosted on the corner of the desk, a posture that made him look both casual and superior. In a moment, he might even crow.

"You and me both," Jep said. "Was there something you needed, or is this a social call?"

"Had to see it with my own eyes. When Lawson agreed to bring you back, I thought I must be dreaming."

"I'm only here to help."

"You sure?"

"There is nothing else on this earth that could have dragged me back here. Trust me."

"I hope that means we can count on you."

"You always could."

"It's too bad your closest allies aren't around to stick up for you anymore. Gill had your back a lot after you left."

"He'll be missed."

"Look, Jep, I don't mean to sound harsh, but we all expect you to carry more than your own weight in this investigation. It's a risk bringing you back, so if you want to change people's minds about you, you're going to have to perform."

"I'm not here to change people's minds. I'm here to get the job done."

"Good." He knocked on the desk to finalize their conversation, then hopped to the floor. Several pairs of eyes returned to their work after he walked away.

"It's hard not to burn bridges when everyone's holding a torch ready to set me on fire." He said it to himself, but Pearce responded.

"They'll cool down once you're settled in."

"We'll see."

"I'll get you those files."

Jep

Pearce entered Lawson's office and clasped his hands behind his back until his boss finished the phone call he was on.

"How's he looking?" Lawson said.

"I think it will work."

"It had better. Everything's riding on Jep's involvement. I hope you've been making yourself amenable to him."

"I haven't been starting a fight, if that's what you mean."

"What's the temperature in the room?"

"There aren't a lot who are happy to have him back."

"Good. Maybe it will encourage him to behave."

"I'd say it will have the opposite effect."

"You'd better hope it doesn't. But the dislike could work in our favor. He wants to choose his own partner. I'd like it to be you. Unless you have a problem with that?"

"None at all. We get along better than any of the other agents so far."

"Good. If he believes he has some kind of connection with you, he'll trust you. I want to know what he's thinking. Where he's heading."

"You don't think he'll share that information with you?"

"Jep has always kept his cards close to his chest. I need an extra pair of eyes."

"That won't be a problem."

"Do whatever you need to do to make sure you're his partner of choice."

"I don't know that he has much of a choice, but I'll continue to support him."

"Good."

"Sir, I want you to know I'm on his side until he proves otherwise. I offered him as an option for a reason. And I'll do whatever is in my power to facilitate his success."

"You say that now, but you don't know him like I do."

"I'm willing to overlook some difficulties. Right now, the objective has to outweigh our personal feelings."

"You think it's my feelings that are hurt by his return?"

"All I mean is that making his life hell won't help him to do what needs to be done."

"You don't have to worry about me. I'll give him a wide berth. My guess is, he'll dig his own grave. Then I can be rid of him once and for all."

Chapter 7

JEP STOOD at the elevator bay with his leather jacket hanging from one hand and his helmet from the other while he watched the numbers change.

"Hold the elevator!" someone shouted as the doors opened.

Jep turned to see Pearce jogging over and leaned against the frame until he got on.

"Welcome officially to the team," Pearce said as they rode up.

Jep had taken several days to study the files as well as make arrangements for his shop to continue operating before returning today.

He'd remained in contact with Pearce, who had filled in the gaps, but a lot of questions were still unanswered. There was no doubt that the case was an unusual one. It felt an awful lot like they were being fed exactly what the enemy wanted them to hear. If they were going to get ahead of these guys, whoever they were, they'd have to start looking from a different perspective. That wouldn't be easy for most of these guys.

"*Back* to the team," Jep said as the doors slid shut.

"Right. Back. I hope I was able to answer all of your questions satisfactorily."

"You did your best." When Jep saw the wary look on Pearce's face, he added, "I mean, it's a tricky case. There's not a lot of information to go on."

"That's true. Usually we're sifting through piles of details, trying to figure out what's relevant and what's not." The elevator doors opened, and Pearce followed Jep to his desk. "Do you have any initial thoughts?"

Jep deposited his helmet under his desk and draped his jacket across the back of his chair before pulling the paperwork out of his backpack.

"My main concerns," he said as he tossed the files onto his desk, "are the gaps."

"What gaps?"

"The wide gaping holes in the reports."

"We've put in everything we have."

"That's disappointing."

"If you're concerned about the data in the reports, Sylvia Gardener is the one to see. She's head of analytics. She can answer any questions you have."

"Gardener?"

Pearce pointed toward her office. "Straight through there. She can be prickly, but she'll help you if she can. Would you like to speak to her now?"

"Actually, no. I'd like to have a look at the site of each of the incidents from the past several months. The last one was the only one in which any agents were injured?"

"Yes. And most of our leads are dead ends."

"Dead ends or dead agents. Not a great starting place."

"That's the reason you're here."

Jep sifted through the files and pulled one out, handing it to Pearce. "What about this one?"

"What about it?" Pearce thumbed through the pages.

"No survivors."

"Them not us. That's where we got our biggest lead."

"The one that led our agents to their doom."

Pearce's eyes lifted to him. "Yes."

"The autopsies suggested some of them were dead for a few days already."

"That's correct."

"I couldn't find any follow up on that."

"There was nothing to follow up."

"Dead people with no explanation gave you nothing to follow up?"

"Like I said. We've had a lot of dead ends."

"Then that's where I'll start, but I should get my partner sorted first. Also, I'll need a vehicle. I only have my bike here."

"No problem. I'll organize the car, and all you have to do is let Lawson know who you're taking with you. Who's the lucky guy?"

"Emery Chapman."

"Emery?"

"Yeah."

"She's not a field agent, she's an analyst."

"I know."

"You need to choose an agent."

"That wasn't the deal. You heard Lawson. He said I could choose whoever I wanted."

Pearce slowly placed the file on Jep's desk. "I don't think that's what he meant. There are plenty of very experienced agents to choose from."

"I know. I still want Emery."

"I can't say how she'll feel about that."

"You haven't even asked her," Jep said.

"You really want to start things off this way?"

"What way? Being unconventional?"

Pearce waited a beat before he said, "That's not what this is."

"Why don't you tell me what you think it is?"

"I can't say for certain. You're either looking for a partner who won't be able to stand up to you, or you're being difficult to see how we'll all react."

"I won't give Emery any reason to need to stand up to me, and I'm not being difficult. I'm making the best call for this investigation."

"You'll have to give me a minute to consult with Lawson."

"You do what you need to do."

"I'll be right back."

Jep glanced across the room at Emery. She was focused on her computer. If she'd noticed him come in, she hadn't given any hint of it.

Jep

He drummed his fingers on the desk, then looked at his watch before checking Lawson's door.

He didn't have to wait long before Lawson marched out of his office with Pearce following. "What's this I hear about your choice of partner?"

"You said I could choose, and I did," Jep said. "I don't understand why there's a problem." He remained composed, a look of confusion rather than anger on his face to keep things civil.

Lawson's already pink face reddened. "And I told Agent Pearce that he must have misunderstood. There's no way you asked for Miss Chapman as a partner." Lawson's voice boomed. "That would be absurd."

"You may want to choose your words more carefully," Jep said as he glanced at Emery. She was staring at them. He nodded in her direction, then looked back at Lawson. "I think she heard you. And unless you have more than one Emery Chapman in the office, she's the one."

"I'm sorry," Lawson said, "but that's out of the question. She's not trained for the field. Are you trying to make a mockery of this organization?"

"Miss Chapman is very professional. I highly doubt she would be an embarrassment."

"You know what I mean."

"She's had no training whatsoever?"

"She's had no experience in the field."

"I don't need her to do any acrobatics."

"What's the point of having her for a partner if you have to babysit?"

Jep pushed his tongue into his cheek. He hoped Emery hadn't heard that.

"What about Pearce?" Lawson said. "You two seem to get along well. Or at least better than the others. Miss Chapman will be uncomfortable with this arrangement."

"Why don't we ask her?" Jep had no way to know how she'd react. She'd probably refuse, but as far as he could see, she was the best person for the job even if they couldn't see it.

"Miss Chapman?" Lawson called her over with a wave of the hand. People in this office liked to wave at her to give orders. If it bothered her, she didn't act like it.

Emery hurried over but remained as far from Jep as possible. "Yes, sir?" She clasped her hands behind her back.

"Mr. Booth—"

"Agent," Jep said with a smile.

"Agent Booth was given permission to choose his partner."

"Yes," Emery said. "I remember him asking."

"He's chosen you."

Jep didn't know how she managed it, but her expression remained unchanged besides the color of her cheeks tinging with pink.

She looked at him. "While I appreciate the offer, unfortunately, I am not a field agent and must therefore decline."

"Need I say more?" Lawson said.

"You told me I could have whatever partner I wanted," Jep said. If he budged on this, they'd expect him to fold on everything else.

"Whatever *agent* you chose," Lawson said.

"That's not what we agreed."

"I'm sorry, but there's no way around it."

Jep pulled his helmet from under his desk and stood. "Thank you for this opportunity, but if you can't keep your word, I can't help you."

He skirted around Pearce, but Emery tripped forward, blocking his way. "I'll do it," she said before clearing her throat. "If that's the only way to get you to stay, then I'll do it. But only for the good of the agency. I'd like my objection noted and that Agent Booth acknowledges that I am not trained to perform the duties required of an agent."

"Noted," Jep said. "And yes, I acknowledge you have not been trained as a field agent and further add that I do not require your skills as such."

"Em, you don't have to do this," Pearce said low.

"I know." She shifted stiffly.

Lawson's sigh rumbled into a low growl. "Fine, but you watch yourself with him, Miss Chapman. And let Gardener know she'll be down an analyst."

He gave one last scowl to Jep, his eyebrows merging into one, before returning to his office.

"There's time to back out if you want to." Pearce said to her. "No one's forcing you to do this."

She looked at Jep. "We all have to make sacrifices."

"Excellent," Jep said. "I'm glad we're finally all in agreement. Pearce, weren't you going to see about organizing a car for me?"

"Yeah." He looked more miserable about this arrangement than anyone. "I'll get right on that." He glanced at Emery before walking away.

"So," she said to Jep. "What now?"

He looked down at her outfit. "I don't suppose you have a change of clothes?"

"What for? We're not riding on your motorcycle."

"We could if you want."

"No, thanks."

"Still, you might be more comfortable in something a little more casual."

"I'm a professional. I like to dress like one."

If her barbs hadn't all been fired in his direction, he would have been impressed. He just wished she'd stand up for herself to the others like she did to him. He was secure enough to let her practice on him if it gave her confidence.

"Okay," he said. "But don't say I didn't warn you."

"Thank you for your concern. Now, if you'll excuse me, I have to inform my supervisor that she'll be short staffed for the foreseeable future."

"Don't worry. It'll be worth it. I promise."

"I won't hold my breath." She turned on her heel and walked away with her back straight.

Jep was sure she'd stopped breathing. And now that he was on his own again, he began second guessing his choice. He had his reasons for singling her out, and they were good ones, but they would all be for nothing if she didn't trust him.

It was clear Pearce had expected to be the chosen one, and he wouldn't have been a bad pick. In fact, he was the obvious choice. But obvious wouldn't cut it in this investigation. Pearce was on the team that had been hunting these guys, and they'd made no headway. He needed a play from left field. If the enemy was reading them, he needed to change the language.

He continued to watch Emery until she reached Gardener's office and turned to look at him.

He lifted his eyebrows in question, and she lowered hers into a frown before turning back.

This would be an interesting experiment.

Chapter 8

EM SMILED at Gardener as she entered her office but could feel Jep's eyes on her. She didn't have time to contemplate his motives or why he wanted her to change her clothes. Did he want her to don leather pants and a tight top? He might be comfortable dressing like a slob, but she never would be. At least she'd said how she felt. Whatever it was about Jep that gave her the courage to speak her mind, she'd welcome it. God often used fire to refine his children. She'd take the challenge head on.

"Sorry to interrupt," she said when Gardener looked up. "I just need a minute."

Sylvia leaned back away from her computer. "Is everything okay? You look upset."

"Do I?"

"Yeah."

"Do you mind if I sit?"

"Not at all."

"It's about the new agent. Jep Booth."

"I haven't had the pleasure," she said, not hiding her disdain. "Not this time, anyway."

"I didn't even think of that. You've been here long enough. You would have worked with him before."

"Yes, but fortunately, we didn't have a lot of contact. He was a very divisive figure in the office, from what I remember. I was surprised not only that he was asked back but that he agreed to come."

"Yeah, well, he made some stipulations for his return. One of them was that he could choose his own partner."

"If he can find one who will agree to ride with him. I can't imagine there would be many."

"Pearce would have if he was asked."

"Who'd he choose?"

"Me."

"Pardon?"

"Out of all the competent agents in the office, he chose me."

"But you're not an agent."

"I know!" Em threw her hands in the air, then collected them back in her lap. "Sorry."

Gardener huffed. "How'd he take it?"

"Take what?"

"When you said no."

"He said he'd leave if I wouldn't be his partner, so I've agreed."

"What? No. That's out of the question. He can't coerce you into accepting. Lawson wouldn't hear of it. Does he even know?"

"He was there. But I offered to go along with it

because we need Agent Booth. Or at least, that's how it appears."

"Do we need him that badly?"

"You heard Truman."

"I did." Gardener pressed her lips together. "So, this is where we're at?"

"I'm afraid so. You're going to be down an analyst for now."

"Then the only thing we can do is make the most of a bad situation."

"How do we do that?"

"We use your position to our advantage."

"I'm all for that, but I don't see how. I don't even really understand why he would choose me over someone like Pearce."

"Maybe it doesn't matter. Whatever made him choose you, it means you'll be there on the front lines. You'll have access to information we only get after the fact in reports from the agents."

"I hadn't thought about it like that."

"It could turn out to be a significant benefit. I've known you long enough, Em. You can handle the pressure. And you'll see firsthand what you've always only read about."

"But will that make a difference to our analysis?"

"Absolutely. It's a dream come true having one of my best on site. There's no middleman."

"I guess that's true."

"It was a good move going along with this. I want you to report back to me everything you and Agent Booth discover. Every detail. I want to know your movements and what he's thinking. Get inside his head if you can, but be careful. I expect he'll put his own spin on what he finds, which makes this even more crucial."

"Wow, yeah. That's true. I can make sure he's bringing back the facts."

"We don't know if he has another agenda, but if he does, we'll know immediately. Em. this is the best thing that could have happened."

"Thank you. You've really helped me get my head around it. I do wish I understood why he chose me though."

"My best guess is it's because you're pretty. He probably thinks you'll be a nice distraction while he's back. And also you're an analyst, so you won't have any input. He expects to act like he's working alone. He'll walk all over you if you let him, and he'll probably attempt to charm you. It's up to you to resist."

"You don't have to worry about that. But if he crosses a line, I'll report him."

"Of course. And that's the right thing to do. But better if it doesn't come to that. If he knows you're not interested, I doubt he'll pursue that line. All you have to do is be a fly on the wall. If he forgets you're there, even better. Be all eyes and ears. And remember, I want to know everything."

"Yeah. I won't miss a thing."

"Good. And don't forget, I'm behind you one hundred percent. You have any trouble, you come to me first. Let me deal with it."

"Thank you." She had been anxious about telling Gardener the mess she'd gotten herself into, but her boss had turned everything around. And it was the most positive interest she'd gotten from her since starting with the task force. She'd been praying that their relationship would strengthen.

Your ways are higher than my ways. She smiled as the verse came to mind.

"I would hope it goes without saying," Gardener said, "that you're still under my charge, even while you're with him. I consider you to be my responsibility."

"I understand."

"Good. Now go out there and do what I know you can."

"Thank you. Again. You've been very helpful."

After collecting her purse from the back of her chair, she stopped by the bathroom and checked the stalls to confirm she was alone before she called her aunt.

"Everything okay?" Carla said.

"More or less. I'm being sent out into the field with a man I don't trust."

"Wait. What? I didn't know you did work outside the office."

"I don't. There's this new guy—actually, he's not new. He used to work here. Then he was asked to leave. Long story, but he's been asked to come back because we need the help, and I've been stuck with him as his partner."

"That sounds…unconventional."

"It is. Analysts don't go out into the field. He'll probably leave me in the car while he does whatever it is he's going to do."

"Then why partner with you if he's not going to use you?"

"Good question."

"Is he cute?"

"Did you seriously just ask me that?"

"You know how I like to lighten the mood when you're tense."

"People's appearances change as you get to know them."

"So he is then?"

"Most women would probably find him attractive, yes."

"But not you?"

"He's not my type. Besides, you're the one always saying stupid things like, 'find someone with whom you are equally yoked.'"

"You think that's stupid?"

"No. But it sounds weird when you say it." Em reapplied her lipstick, then rubbed her lips together.

"But it's true."

"Yes. And it is what I want. However, Jep is definitely not that guy."

"I didn't ask if you were going to marry him. I asked if he was good looking."

"He rides a motorcycle, and he's got a couple of tattoos. He's dark and brooding and demanding, and he thinks he can have whatever he wants."

"Sounds sexy."

"Oh my goodness. I can't believe you said that."

"What? I'm just trying to establish if he's attractive, and you're making it difficult."

"Why? What difference does it make?"

"It doesn't, but your life is more interesting than mine."

"My life is not that interesting."

"That's not how it sounds from where I'm standing."

"I don't expect it will last long. The assistant director doesn't even like him. They had some kind of falling out years ago, although I don't know why yet."

"Yet?"

"I'm hoping to find out so I know how bad things really are."

"Now I'm confused."

"About what?"

"Why is he even there?" Carla said.

"It came from the top. The deputy director. But this guy could be the only answer to the difficulties we're facing in our latest case. That's why I'm determined to make the most of it."

"Good for you. But make sure you stick up for yourself. Let him know where you stand from the start. If he thinks he's going to get you into bed with him—"

"Carla."

"What? You said he's not a great guy. That goes with certain connotations. It's in your best interest to make sure he understands from the start that that is not a road he should even contemplate taking."

"I understand what you're saying. I need to be on the offense with him. Not the defense."

"Exactly."

"I haven't had any trouble speaking my mind before. I'm not going to start now."

"Since when do you speak your mind at work?"

"I do with him."

"Really? You've already had words?"

"I don't know why, but as intimidating as he seems, I'm always on the front foot with him."

"Wow. The new you. Sounds like God's opening the right doors. You've been too comfortable sitting at your desk anyway. It's the perfect time to try something new."

"I could use a positive change. But please be praying for me because I am way out of my depth."

"Definitely. And good luck."

"Thanks. I've gotta go. He's probably waiting."

"Let me know how things go."

"I will."

Jep started the car and looked down at Emery's lap, where her fists were kneading her legs.

"Everything okay?" he said.

"Yeah, I just…" She took a deep breath. "I won't sleep with you."

"Excuse me?"

"I wanted you to know that from the start. In case that's why you chose me as a partner. If you thought you could have a bit of fun while you're here, you chose the wrong person."

He had shifted into drive, but he put it back into park. "Look, Em. Emery. I know there's a lot of gossip around the office about my time here before. Some of it's probably true. But I have never treated any woman disrespectfully. You can ask Lawson if you don't want to take my word for it. He doesn't like me for a lot of reasons, but that's not one of them."

She chewed on her lip for a second.

"What is it?" Jep said. "You want to say something? Let's hear it."

"Why me?"

"Ah yes. The question on everyone's mind."

"If you think I'll sit quietly and let you do whatever you want. If that's your reasoning..." Her face reddened. "I will. You can consider me invisible. I won't complain about anything as long as you don't put me in a compromising position. But do me the courtesy of being straight about your motives. Other than that—" She zipped her lips.

Jep sighed. He knew she wouldn't believe him if he told her. She'd made that clear the other day at the park. He'd have to show her.

"You want to know why I chose you?" He put the car back into drive and pulled out of the parking spot. "I'll show you."

"Where are we going?"

"Downtown."

"Why?"

"You'll see when we get there."

Chapter 9

WHEN JEP PULLED over on a wide, dingy street, Emery thought he was going to check his phone for directions. But then he put the car in park and looked at her.

"This is it?" she said, glancing out the window at the illegal transactions of both drugs and flesh occurring in broad daylight.

"Yeah."

"Where are we?"

"Maddison Boulevard."

"I know what street we're on. I read the sign at the intersection. What I want to know is where we are with regards to the investigation. Maddison Boulevard wasn't in any of the reports."

His eyes squinted in skepticism. "You couldn't possibly know that for sure."

"I have a good memory."

"That good?"

She thought back to her encounter with Gardener

over her misremembered details. She hadn't been wrong, but her memory wasn't what she'd thought it was. "It's not flawless. Do you have a contact here or something? And what does it have to do with choosing me as a partner?"

"Tell me what you see."

She stared at him for a second. When he didn't say more, she said, "I don't understand."

"Look out the window." He pointed across the road. "And tell me what you see."

"Is this a test?"

"If that's what it takes to get your cooperation."

"What if I fail?"

"It's not that kind of test."

She took her time doing what he asked. He'd given her no hint about what she was supposed to be looking for. "I can see a couple of drug deals going on. Prostitutes. Homelessness."

"What else?"

"I don't know—an abandoned building. Overflowing garbage can. There's a twenty-four-hour convenience store that looks like it's seen better days. A sign says the corn chips are on sale, but judging but the faded coloring, it's a sign that's no longer relevant."

"What else?"

"You want more?"

"You haven't seen everything there is to see."

"I'm not trained in the field. You want a crime being committed? I already mentioned the drugs."

"That's not what I'm after."

"I don't know how to spot what it is you're looking for. I'm an analyst."

"Then analyze."

She relented. "Uh…" Scanning the faces, she looked for one that stood out. "That girl over there." The prostitute was petite with bleached blonde hair and purple eyelids heavy with eyeliner.

"Which one?" Jep said.

"With the tasseled skirt, who doesn't look like she's old enough to be out here."

"I see her."

"I think she's pregnant."

His eyes shifted from the girl to Em. "Why?"

"I don't know."

"Yes, you do."

She huffed. "I guess it's because of the way she holds herself. She's touched her stomach a couple of times, and when she does, her face changes."

Jep looked back, and he watched for a minute. "I see what you mean. Do you think she wants to keep it?"

"How would I know that?"

"I asked what you thought, not what the absolute truth was."

"Then I *think* it's complicated."

"How so?"

"Why are you asking me all of this? What does this have to do with the case?"

"Nothing."

"Then why are we here?"

"You wanted to know why I chose you."

"This isn't answering that question."

"It won't if you keep interrupting."

"You said I couldn't fail, but I don't believe you." She crossed her arms.

"You think I brought you out here to prove that you aren't cut out to be my partner?"

"Maybe."

"Then why would I pick you in the first place?"

"I don't know." She huffed again. "Fine." Then she looked back at the girl. Her plan to be strong was quickly disintegrating.

A car pulled up in front of the girl, and a homeless man standing in the alcove of an empty building straightened, watching the exchange.

"Are you this difficult with Pearce?" Jep said.

"What?"

"Pearce. Do you give him a hard time too?"

"He's never taken me into the field."

"He did when you came to get me, and you did exactly as you were told."

She frowned. "That's different."

He leaned toward her only a fraction, but it felt a lot closer. "Emery. Tell me why it's complicated with the girl."

"If I do, can we leave?"

"That depends on your answer."

She looked back out the window. "I think she wants to get rid of it, but she also doesn't. A job like she has would be tough with a baby to look after. But the idea of…her other option…is heartbreaking for her—also, that homeless guy to the left of her—"

"The one sitting in the doorway?"

"Yeah. With the beard. I'm pretty sure he knows."

"Why?"

"He's protective of her, although I can't be sure for what reason exactly. Whether for good or for bad. Maybe he's the father, or maybe he's just looking out for her." She shook her head. "Poor thing. I can't imagine what her life must be like or what led her to this."

"You want to see if she wants help?" Jep said. His voice had softened.

"What do you mean?"

"I don't know how else to say it. I have some contacts that can help her if she wants it. You want to ask?"

"Me?"

"Yeah."

"Now?"

"Why not?"

"What does this have to do with terrorists or—wait. Let me guess. Nothing?"

"Right now, we're here to see if that girl wants our help. If you want."

"I wouldn't know what to say."

"All you can do is ask, and I'll be there to back you up."

She looked out at the girl, and her throat tightened. It was easy to turn aside and say the problem was too hard. But the truth was she was terrified to ask. She'd joined the agency to help people and make a difference. But when it came to the basics, she was too scared.

"She looks so young." Em made a face of indecision. "You'll come with me?"

"Absolutely."

She plucked at her silk blouse. "I'm overdressed."

"That's why I thought you might want to change."

"So you did have a legitimate reason."

"I hate to imagine what you were thinking."

She opened her mouth to apologize but closed it again. Jep may not be who she'd thought he was, but she needed more evidence before she would commit.

After giving her shirt another tug, she said, "If we're going to do this, we'd better go now before I change my mind."

"Great. Let's go."

She waited a beat to let him get out of the car before her, but he let her cross the street first.

Em hurried up to the girl, trying not to think about how she and Jep approaching her would look.

She glanced back to make sure Jep was with her. He gave her an encouraging smile. Then she turned back. "Excuse me," she said when she reached the gutter. The homeless man at the building stood but remained in the door.

"What'd *you* want?" the girl said, giving Em a thorough looking over before she turned her attention to Jep and smiled innocently. "I think I know what *you* want."

Em looked back at Jep, who had his eyes firmly on her and continued to smile that same warm smile.

She lowered her voice before she spoke to the girl again. "I was, uh, wondering. I was wondering if you wanted—uh—help."

"With what?" the girl said. "You want to share makeup tips? I could show you a thing or two. You look

Jep

like you could use some loosening up. Spice up things with your boyfriend here. I think he'd like it."

"He's not—I thought that maybe with your—you know." She nodded toward the girl's stomach. Up close, it was impossible to tell her age. She could have been anywhere between fifteen and twenty-five.

The girl's face hardened. "With my what?"

"Your baby. I was wondering if you wanted help. We might be able to help you keep it."

The girl took a step back. "How do you know about that?"

Em licked her lips. "Do you want to keep it?"

"That's my business, not yours. So unless your boyfriend is looking for a good time, you can get lost."

The homeless man stumbled forward. "What's going on?" he slurred. The smell of booze on him was strong. When he tried to move closer to Em, Jep stepped in his way.

"We don't want any trouble," Jep said. "We're just trying to see if the lady would like some help."

"From you?" He spit at Jep's feet. "You probably wanna cut her up into little pieces for your own amusement. Everyone always wants a piece of Starla. Well, you can get lost."

"We'll go when Starla asks us to go."

"Then I'm asking you to," Starla said. "I don't want your kind of help."

"You heard her," the man said. "Get outta here before I make you."

"Okay," Jep said. "If she's sure."

"She's sure." The man stumbled closer. "I'm sure."

Em looked at the girl, and her heart broke. She'd lived a life that taught her not to trust people. "Please. You need help, and we can do that. You could keep your baby."

"She said no!" the man howled and pulled a knife with surprising speed, thrusting it past Jep and catching Em on the arm.

Jep had him unarmed and in a headlock a fraction of a second later.

"Are you okay?" he said to Em, his eyes wide with fear, or something like it. He didn't notice Starla screaming hysterically and beating on his back. Or the man, who was thrashing and bellowing.

"Let him go!" Starla screeched. "He didn't do anything to you!"

"I'm fine," Em yelled over the noise. She was clutching her arm against her stomach. "Please, let's go. Please."

"We should call the police," he said.

"No. I want to go."

"Enough!" Jep shouted at the girl to startle her into submission. "Back off so I can let your friend go." She gave him a hard shove but then tripped back, and Jep slowly released the man. "My friend was only trying to help your friend," Jep said to him, keeping his distance.

The man sneered. "If I see you around here again, I'll make sure you can never leave."

Jep put his arm around Em and led her back to the car. Once she was in her seat, he quickly got in and drove around the corner, where he parked again and tugged gently on her arm.

"Let me see," he said. She slowly relinquished it but looked away while he assessed the damage. It wasn't that she was squeamish about a cut, but the whole event had made her body tingle all over, and she was lightheaded.

He unbuttoned her cuff and rolled up the bloody sleeve. "It's deep."

"Shouldn't we keep it covered?" Em said. "I could get blood in the car."

"I doubt it would be the first time. How're you feeling? You look pale."

"I'll be okay. I'm just shaken up a little."

"Unfortunately, there's no way to know what was on that knife. I'll take it in to be analyzed, but they'll want to give you some shots at the hospital, and they'll do tests to be sure."

"You still have the knife?"

"Of course I do." He reached for his bag in the back seat and pulled out a T-shirt. "It's clean," he said as he wrapped it around her arm. "Keep pressure on it. You're not feeling dizzy or nauseous?"

"A little."

"Let me know if you think you're going to pass out."

"I'll be okay." She bit the inside of her cheek. "Do you think there was something bad on the knife?"

"I'll make sure they fast track the results."

He was quiet for a few minutes after he pulled back onto the street, his fingers drumming a quick staccato of nervous energy.

"I'm sorry," he finally said. "I should have seen it coming. I thought it would be safe. I never should have — It's my fault."

"It's a shame not everyone wants help."

"I knew it was a possibility. But a guy like that…he was drunk, but I should have known. I thought I had any threat contained. The last thing I wanted to do was put you in danger."

"It's okay."

"No. It's not."

"Minus the knife, it was good for me to step outside of my comfort zone. I've never done anything like that before."

"Which part? Talking to the girl? Or getting stabbed."

"Well…both."

"Doesn't matter. I shouldn't have done it. I made a bad call. I'll choose another partner."

"Why? I mean. You would. I shouldn't have been out there. That's clear. I'm not trained for that. If you had an agent with you who knew what they were doing, that wouldn't have happened. The way you disarmed that guy was impressive."

"Not impressive enough." His face had settled into a deep, regretful frown.

"But I still don't get it."

"What?"

"Why you brought me here. What were you expecting to happen?"

"Oh, that. I wanted to show you what you could do."

"So I *did* fail."

"Not at all. You were amazing. Exactly what I expected. The problem was, I could see how badly you wanted to help that girl, and I got caught up in the moment."

"I'm confused. What did I do that was amazing?"

"Do you remember the drive back from my place the day you and Pearce came to get me?"

"Vividly."

"You saw what was going to happen in the park before it happened."

"You mean that fight you stopped?"

"Yeah."

"All I remember is you threatening to jump out of a moving vehicle."

"Before that."

"Before that, we were driving down the street." Her arm was beginning to throb. "I think my adrenaline is wearing off."

"It's not much farther to the hospital. You think you can hang on a little longer?"

"Yeah, it's just aching."

"So you really don't remember?"

"Remember what?"

"Your reaction," Jep said.

"I honestly have no idea what you're talking about."

"In the car. You were looking into the park, and you saw it."

"Only because you jumped out and took off after those guys."

"The only reason I saw them was because I responded to you. You saw it first. That's why I acted."

She frowned. "I don't know what you think you saw—"

"Think back. The car was quiet. You were looking out the window. You saw something."

She put the details back into place. Put herself back in the car to the time before the focus was on Jep.

"I did see them," she said, picturing the posture she'd noticed in the two older men. But she'd dismissed it like she'd almost dismissed the pregnant girl. It wasn't something she thought she could influence. By the time Jep had responded, she'd put it out of her mind. "You're saying you noticed my reaction? I can't even remember making a move."

"It wasn't much. You stiffened."

"That's it?"

"That's all it took."

She could feel her pulse in her arm, the pain increasing with each beat.

"That's why I chose you as a partner," he said. "I need someone who can discern what's going on besides the obvious. Most agents wouldn't have picked up on the pregnant girl. They would have been too busy watching the drug deals or something else. They would have focused on the homeless man as a threat and not on what his motivation was."

"But how does that help the investigation?"

"If we're going to catch these guys, we can't look at them the same as before. When I went through those reports, what I noticed was that, whoever is behind this, they know how we operate. They know our response time and our playbook, and they've been using it against us. I don't need a field agent with on-the-job-training. I need someone who doesn't have any of that but has the instincts to see what's between the lines. Not to mention your memory for the details."

"Oh."

"That's what I was thinking anyway. I guess you instinctively knew it wasn't a good idea to be my partner, but I refused to accept it. I accept it now."

She scrunched up her face against the prodding headache that was digging its fingers into her temple. If it wasn't for the pain, she could focus more clearly. Everything she'd thought about Jep was now turned on its head.

She'd agreed to partner with him as a last resort. Him giving her a way out of it was something she should jump on, but now that she knew the truth, she didn't know what to do. But she couldn't ignore the fact that she wasn't cut out for field work. He couldn't do his job if he was spending the whole time protecting her from every possible threat. The advantages he saw in her must have diminished considerably. Their ceasing their partnership was probably best for them both.

Chapter 10

JEP TOUCHED her elbow to lead her onto the elevator back at the office.

"I'm sorry about your shirt, too," he said.

"I've got more. Next time, I'll take your advice."

When the doors opened on the fifth floor, Lawson was waiting.

"Miss Chapman," he said, closing in on her. "I take it you're reasonably okay?"

"Yeah." She lifted her arm to show off the bandage. "Seven stitches later. Not too bad, considering."

He glanced at Jep, then back at her. "Good. Why don't you take a few days off. You've earned it."

"For a cut on my arm? I see others in the team come in with a lot worse."

"As an analyst, I have no expectation of you overcoming an experience like that to get right back to work. That attack must have been terrifying."

"It—well—no. Jep was there. I was shaken up by it,

Jep

but that's to be expected." It hadn't occurred to her until that moment that she hadn't been scared.

"If he'd done his job properly," Lawson said, breaking her train of thought, "you wouldn't have gotten hurt."

"A few painkillers, and I'm good to go. Really."

"You're sure?"

"Absolutely."

"You're a real trooper. You can let Gardener know you're back on her team. Jep, you can come with me."

"He didn't do anything wrong," Em said. "And I—"

"I have all the information I need. Thank you. If you're staying, you can return to your desk."

"But sir—"

"He said he'd keep you safe, and he didn't. This was exactly what I was afraid of. Jep, come with me."

Em remained in place as Jep followed Lawson to his office.

The door slammed shut, but Lawson's voice still carried through the room. "You might be good on the field, Jep, but you're incapable of working in a team. You not only refused to listen to solid advice, but you then put Miss. Chapman's life in danger for what? To prove a point? You're a disgrace. And I'm sickened by the prospect of having you in this office."

There was a pause. If Jep was speaking, she couldn't hear it.

"This must be your first work injury," Pearce said.

"I got a paper cut once." She laughed weakly, her attempt to make light of the situation failing to lighten her mood.

"I'm sorry it happened."

"It's no one's fault. These things happen."

"No, they don't. Not when he was supposed to be keeping you away from anything dangerous, and what does he do?"

"It's not what you think. Jep's a good guy. Maybe he does bother some agents by the way he works, but his motivation is all good."

"You sure about that?"

"I'm positive."

"Okay. I'll take your word for it. I just hope he doesn't still expect you to be his partner."

"No. He apologized for that."

"That's one positive outcome from all of this."

They both looked to Lawson's office when his door opened, but Jep stopped and turned back into the room when Lawson spoke again.

"While I try to get my orders to have you here reversed, I am taking back control. You can sit at your desk and write up a report about today's incident, and then you can write another report about how you would behave differently so that it never happens again. You will remain in this office until I know what to do with you."

Jep shook his head and walked to his desk without looking at anyone.

The room remained silent as he tossed his badge on his desk and laid his weapon beside it before collecting his things. He looked around until he spotted Emery, and he walked over to her.

"I'm really sorry," he said. "The thing I regret the

Jep

most about coming back is what happened to you. You won't have to worry about it happening again."

He didn't bother with the elevator. Instead, he yanked open the emergency door, causing the alarm to sound. He jerked to a stop and looked up, obviously not expecting that, then walked through the door and disappeared.

Em was frozen in place while a few scrambled and made phone calls to get the alarm turned off.

When the silence returned, a gaping hole appeared in its place.

"It wasn't his fault," she said to Pearce. "It really wasn't. It would have been so much worse if he hadn't been there."

"But you have to understand Lawson's position. You never should have been there in the first place."

She turned on him. "Then wrap me in cotton wool, why don't you?"

"Em—"

"No, we could have gotten in a car accident because of someone else's driving, and Lawson would have blamed Jep. He was waiting for any opportunity to get rid of him. So was everyone."

"Not everyone. He has some friends in here."

"Does he? You mean all those people who kept him from walking out the door?"

"You say that like you wanted him to stay. I thought you didn't like the guy."

"I—I was wrong about Jep, and I don't want to lose this task force. I think we can do some real good here."

"Then let me put your mind at ease. What

happened between Agent Booth and the assistant director was always going to happen. Those two needed to blow off steam at each other. I'm sure Jep will be back once he's cooled off. He's got a taste for it now. Trust me. I know the feeling. Tomorrow or a few days from now, he'll turn up back here like nothing happened."

"And Lawson will be fine with that?"

"He'll have to be."

"Maybe you should go talk to him."

"Jep or Lawson?"

"Both. You seem to be the only tie those two have. If anyone can mend this, you can."

"There's nothing to do right now. They need to cool off. Trust me. Jep will be back, and Lawson will take him."

"I hope you're right."

The elevator doors opened, and Emery swallowed a tiny gulp of air, but it wasn't Jep. It hadn't been all week.

"Hey, Pearce," she said as he walked past.

"What's up?"

"Jep hasn't come back."

"No."

"Are you still confident he will?"

He thought about it for a minute. "I honestly thought he'd be back by now."

"Do you know if Lawson has told the deputy director yet?"

"He's been putting it off."

"Truman won't be happy to find out he's the last to know."

"He's got bigger issues at the moment. He's currently testifying at a congressional hearing, so Lawson can avoid it until that's finished."

"And then what?"

"I don't know."

"You should call him. Jep, I mean."

"I have."

She jerked forward. "You did? What did he say?"

"When he finally answered after I called him a half a dozen times, he said—and I quote—'Never going to happen.' He obviously needs more time to cool down than I anticipated."

"It sounds to me like he's made up his mind. I wonder if—" She shook the thought away.

"What? If you have an idea, you had better share it. We need a miracle here."

"I was thinking, maybe I could call him. Now that my arm is healing and I've been cleared of any other ailments emanating from it, maybe that would soften the ground for his return."

"You'd feel comfortable doing that?"

"Comfortable? No. It will definitely be awkward. I barely know the guy. But if it would help, it's worth a shot."

Pearce let out a relieved sigh. "Honestly, I'd hoped you'd offer. I didn't want to ask after everything that's happened, but I think we'd have a better chance of him listening if it's coming from you. Whatever it is he sees in you, you may be the only one who can bring him back."

She got stuck on his "*whatever it is he sees in you*" comment for a second. "Okay. If that's what it will take, I'll call him."

Pearce winced.

"What?" Em said.

"I hate to ask…"

"What?"

"He avoided most of my calls. I think if you went to see him, you'd have a better chance. A phone call is too easy to dismiss, but if you're standing there in front of him…"

"A phone call was one thing, but a visit? You want me to go to his workshop? Alone?"

"Is that too much to ask? It's too much to ask. Forget it."

"It's just…wouldn't it be weird for me to turn up at his place? Wouldn't it seem…I don't know…desperate?"

"Aren't we?"

"What if you came with me."

"I could, but I think it would mean more if you turned up alone. You said you'd changed your mind about him. And he's probably defensive right now. I know *I* would be. We don't want anything to get in the way of his favorable response."

The thought of turning up on his doorstep made her cringe, but she didn't know why. He thought better of her than most of the people in the office.

"Are you embarrassed by the idea?" Pearce said.

"Why would I be embarrassed?"

"Using your feminine touch to sway him."

"That's not what I would do."

"Then what's holding you back?"

"Nothing. Okay. I'll do it."

"Fantastic. Thank you." He pressed his palms together in gratitude.

"But I have a condition."

"I think Jep rubbed off on you. Let's hear it."

"If I go talk to Jep, you have to talk to Lawson. I don't want to go through the hard work of getting him back in the office only to lose him again because Lawson can't rein his temper in."

"Done. You can leave Lawson to me."

"You have to make sure that Lawson will continue to agree with Jep's original terms."

"Absolutely, but while you're with Jep, confirm that he intends to choose another partner."

"I can still be his partner if he wants."

"What? No way."

"Why not?"

He pointed at her arm. "That, for one."

"That was unforeseen."

"What happened to you only being his partner because it was the only way to make him stay? Surely he doesn't expect to continue with that arrangement."

"He doesn't. And maybe he won't want me anymore. I doubt he does. But I'm okay with it if that's what it takes to get him back."

"You're a tougher woman than I ever gave you

credit for. What about Gardener? She may refuse to let you out of her sight."

"She won't. She turned out to be quite agreeable to having one of her analysts in the field."

"That doesn't surprise me. Well, if your boss is okay with it, then I guess I have to go along with it."

"Then we're agreed?"

"If you're sure."

"I am." She tugged at her skirt. "When do you think I should go?"

"The sooner the better. What are you up to now? If Gardener is on board, you won't have any trouble getting out of work. And you can take one of our cars. I'll clear it."

"Thanks. But—"

"What?"

"What do I say to a man like Jep to convince him to do something he doesn't want to do?"

"You're assuming he doesn't want to come back."

"Isn't that why he left?"

"He left because Lawson took away his freedom. He came to work here because he wanted to. You just have to remind him of that."

"Right."

"Any more questions?"

"A million but none you can answer. I guess I'll wing it."

"Good luck."

So that was it. She was going to go see Jep. A man she barely knew, but who seemed to know her. And she was going to convince him to come back. Unless she couldn't.

God, what have you gotten me into? Or is this my own doing? It was impossible to tell.

Chapter 11

EMERY WAS DRIVING out of the city when her phone rang. "Aunt Carla. To what do I owe the pleasure?"

"You want to know the real reason I want you to drop the 'aunt' part?"

"Why?"

"Because it makes me feel old."

"You are old." Em laughed at Carla's sputter. "Kidding. Carla. It's nice to hear from you."

"I won't keep you long. I know you're working, but I wanted to see if you have time for a lunch date. We haven't seen much of each other lately. I need some time with my favorite niece named Emery."

"You're worried about me?"

"A little. You get into those phases where you work too hard. Let me see you to reassure myself."

"I'm not overworking myself, but it would still be nice to have lunch. Unfortunately I'm on my way out of the city. But maybe another day?"

"Where are you headed? Or is it a secret?" Her

Jep

voice dropped to a forced whisper. "Are you with that guy? What was his name? Or wait, am I on speaker?"

Em laughed. "You are on speaker, but I'm alone. I will be seeing Jep soon, though. I'm on my way to his place now."

"Whoa, hang on a second. What have I missed?"

"It's business, not pleasure. I'm trying to get him to come back."

"To work?"

"Yes."

"So I *have* missed something."

"We had an incident at work last week, and the assistant director blew up at him, so he quit."

"You never told me that."

"I expected him to return, but he hasn't. I can't say I blame him. If Lawson spoke to me the way he spoke to Jep, I would have burst into tears."

"Yikes. But from what you said about Jep before, it sounded like he had it coming."

"I was wrong. I had Jep all wrong."

"Hang on, let me sit down. This just got interesting."

"If you're going to make fun of me, I'll hang up."

"There's no fun here. I'm intrigued. What did you get wrong?"

"Everything. I barely know the guy, but he understands me better than anyone else in the office—and before you say anything, I stand by my earlier comment that he's not the guy for me."

"Except that he knows you better than anyone else. Right. Got it."

"You know what my non-negotiables are. Besides, I

wouldn't be allowed to date an agent even if I wanted to."

"You said he quit."

"Yeah, but I'm going to see him now and get him to change his mind." The line was silent. "You still there?"

"I'm thinking."

"About?"

"The unexpected turns life takes. You want me to pray for you? You need some wisdom?"

"I'll never say no to prayer. If we don't get him back, I'm pretty sure they'll shut us down."

"You'd lose your job over this?"

"No, but I'll be shifted to another department, and I really like where I work. Also, I'm afraid we'd never get to the bottom of who's doing this, and if we don't…"

"If we don't, what? Something classified will happen?"

"There's the very real possibility of a catastrophic event."

"Oh. Wow. Should I leave town? Should you?"

"As far as we know, there's nothing imminent, but…actually I would feel better if you didn't spend a lot of time in crowds or overpopulated areas."

"That sounds serious."

"I'm being overcautious right now."

"Does this have anything to do with that big explosion a few weeks back? They said it was a gas leak."

"I can't tell you that."

"Got it. I'll stick close to home, and I'll be praying. Good luck."

"Thanks."

Jep

Jep was bent over an engine, tightening a bolt, when Slate craned his neck toward the front of the shop. "Oh my. What have we got here? Whatever she needs, please let me be the one to do the job."

Jep saw the lewd grin. "Stop it." He smacked him in the chest with the wrench and grabbed a rag before moving to the side of the car to see the beautiful woman who had walked in to distract his staff.

He just about had to pick his jaw back up off the floor. "Emery?"

Slate bumped his shoulder. "You know her?"

"No—yeah. I mean…yeah." He wasn't sure what about her presence filled him with so much elation, but he was glad to see her. "She's someone I used to work with."

"You sure? Because your smile says different."

Jep chucked the rag in Slate's face and threaded his way past the clutter to the front.

"Hey, Em—Emery. What are you doing here?"

"You can call me Em."

"What?"

"I know when we first met, I told you to call me Emery, but that was because I didn't know you."

"You mean you didn't like me?"

She grinned. "Call me Em."

He was more glad to see her than he should have been. If he could have nailed down his stomach to keep it from betraying him, he would have. "Em…how's your arm?"

113

"Better. Healing well. And I got the lab results back. I'm all clear."

"Great. That's fantastic. It's been playing on my mind. I wanted to call and ask, but thought you'd prefer me to stay out of your business from now on."

"I don't blame you, you know."

"You'd be the only one."

She looked like she wanted to say more, but she scanned the workshop instead. "Nice place you have here."

"You think so? You like a sagging roof and oil stains?"

"It has its charm. What's back there?" She pointed at the large double doors.

"That's where we paint vehicles. You need a dust-free environment. It's the reason the rest of this place is in such bad shape. I put all my money into setting that up. I'm training a few of the guys. Giving them some skills so they can get their lives together."

"Is he one of them?" She nodded toward Slate, who was watching them, eyes wide in amusement. When Jep turned, Slate ducked out of sight.

"Yeah, that's one of them. He's got a real talent for it, actually."

"Is he getting his life together?"

"He's getting there. If you knew where he started, you'd understand how far he's come."

"Where did he start? If it's okay to ask."

"He got kicked out of his home when he was fourteen because he wouldn't let his uncle keep abusing him.

Jep

Lived a very hard life on the streets for a couple of years until I found him."

She shook her head. "There's so much pain out there."

"There is."

"And you just take these guys in off the street?"

"I have rules and expectations. I've had to turn some of them away. Forcefully remove others. They're rough diamonds, but if I can get through to them, give them a chance they never had, you never know what heights they'll reach. I hope I can at least do some good."

"Is this what you've been doing since you left the agency the first time?"

"Not at the start. I opened up this shop with the last of my savings for something to do, and the boys I didn't run into out on the street turned up at my door. It got out of control, so I had to set some limits, and this whole thing kind of grew from there. I've got a couple of good guys that help me out, and I get donations of old cars and stuff for the boys to practice on."

"That's wonderful. I had no idea."

Jep laughed. "Not many outside my circle do. I know what you first thought of me."

"Then let me be the first to admit I was wrong. About a lot of things."

"I appreciate you saying that."

She picked up a fuel filter and looked it over. "So you're happy here?"

"Happy? That's a tricky question." Best to change the subject. "You have a car that needs servicing?"

"I brought a work car. I think they have someone for that."

"Wow. You confiscated a work car to come see me? How'd you manage that one? Or didn't they know where you were headed?"

"Pearce organized it for me."

"Pearce knew you were coming here, and he let you?"

"He's the one who suggested it."

"Oh." It deflated him a little knowing it wasn't her idea.

"I didn't think you'd be interested in seeing me."

"You're one of the few people I'd be happy to see at my door anytime."

"Even if I told you I'm here to convince you to come back?"

"You said this was Pearce's idea?"

"He said he called you."

"He did. But I find it hard to believe he'd let you within a mile of me. Doesn't everyone at the office think my sole purpose in life is to get you killed?

"No one thinks that. And I came with Pearce's blessing."

"But not Lawson's."

"We're working on him."

"It's good to see you, and I appreciate the effort, but there's no point me coming back if Lawson's going to keep me caged. I won't work under his direction. It wouldn't be good for either one of us."

"Pearce said he'd take care of it. And—" she took a deep breath. "I'll still be your partner if you want."

He chuckled. "Say it like you mean it."

"I *do* mean it. If you still want me. But I'd understand if you'd prefer someone better trained."

He had conflicting emotions he wasn't expecting. "I wouldn't ask that of you. You'd be off the hook. I could probably work okay with Pearce."

"No! I mean. No. I'd like to still be your partner. It's up to you. But if you meant what you said before. Unless…no. You're right. You'd be better off with— whatever. Forget I said anything."

"Are you saying you *want* to be my partner?"

"I— Yes."

"Why?"

"Because. There's no one else in the office who believes in me the way you do. No one else trusts my instincts. To them, all I am is an analyst. I'm not supposed to have gut feelings, and yet, I knew something wasn't right. I knew that the last mission was going to be a disaster."

That got his attention. "You did?"

"Yeah. But I didn't have any data to back up my feelings, so I was dismissed."

"I knew it."

"Knew what?"

"That I'd picked the right partner. How'd you know something was wrong?"

"I told you. I just knew."

"Yeah, but your instincts come from putting together what others don't notice. What did you see that the other's missed?"

"I really don't know this time. I tried to find it

because it would be impossible to convince Gardener or Lawson that there was reason for concern without solid evidence. I spent hours poring through the case files. I had these ghosts of memory about details I thought were there, but then I couldn't find them."

"There were gaps?"

"I don't know. I just…I couldn't find what I thought was there."

"Come with me," he said.

She followed him into his office, where he set up a folding chair for her.

"Is this your office?" she said.

"I know it's a mess. A tidy office space is not my forte. Can I get you anything? Tea, coffee, water?"

"No, I'm fine, thanks. What did you want to show me?"

He pulled a rolling chair from behind his desk and sat close to her. "Tell me what details made you uncomfortable with the operation. I know you said you couldn't find them, but tell me what you expected to find. What were the signs you noticed? Take your time. Think back."

"It started with the previous missions. You know we were getting very little intel, and whenever we did get something, they had already cleared out before we could get there. One time, we were contacted by local police on a B&E that was in progress at a factory, but we missed it."

"Yeah. I read that."

"All of that stuff put together made it look like they knew how we operate."

Jep

"That's exactly what I was thinking. But we did find intel a few times."

"Yeah, that's what I mean. If they knew what we were going to do before we did it, why wouldn't they have removed sensitive information?"

"But what about that time our team did get in? There were no survivors on their side to remove anything."

"That was a weird one."

"Yeah?"

"I was hoping for more on that specifically because I remembered the autopsies being off, but when I went back, the details I thought I'd remembered weren't what I remembered."

"Could the reports have been tampered with?"

"It's unlikely, but anything's possible at this point."

"Who would have access to do that?"

"Who knows? It may not even be sinister if it *did* happen. Sometimes stuff goes missing because someone's taken it out and hasn't put it back yet. Or it could have gotten left in another file."

"But you said the details were different from what you remembered."

"I could have gotten it wrong. I'm not infallible. And if I got a sense of something, that could also have skewed my memory."

"What was off about them?"

"The dead bodies. The ones who were dead before our team got there."

"Yeah. I read about that."

"They identified some of them, but not all."

"I read that as well."

"I looked into a few and came up with some interesting information. Details about them coming into the US and their movements, but it didn't really trigger anything until the pieces started coming together."

"You did some digging? I asked Pearce about that, why they weren't looked into. He said there was nothing to find."

"Yeah. They didn't think it was worth investigating too thoroughly. I only did it because…well, I don't know, I guess because it was strange. The majority of bodies we recovered had been dead for days."

"Why do you think that was? Why would they do that?"

"All I can come up with is they wanted us to think we had a big win so we believed what we found was valuable. When I went back through the autopsy reports, I couldn't find the same information."

"That's significant enough to suggest someone's changed details."

"It's impossible to prove when it can be explained away."

"How?"

"I could have looked up the wrong person. Or if the spelling of the name was wrong at the beginning but was updated. There are so many holes that you can poke through my concerns, it's impossible to get anywhere with it."

"Has an inside man even been considered?"

"It was suggested."

"Was it pursued?"

"Yeah. Quietly. But I'm the newest member. Everyone else on the team has a long record of service."

"That doesn't mean someone hasn't been turned."

"I know. But they've been vetted, and now they've been re-vetted, so if someone is dirty, they've hidden it better than our searching can find."

"It's happened before."

"You really think someone in our office is behind this?" Em shifted uncomfortably.

"We have to consider all the possibilities. Does anyone stand out?"

"No. No one."

"You sure? You haven't noticed anything? No matter how small. Think back to everyone's actions throughout your time with the unit. You've never had a suspicion?"

"No. But I don't know everyone that well. Even my supervisor. And I have to be careful that my personal feelings don't interfere."

"Meaning there are some you don't like?"

"It's not a matter of not liking. Lawson's not the easiest person to get along with, and my supervisor can be cold and dismissive, but that's not enough to raise a red flag."

"If it's not someone within the task force now, maybe it's someone who has been before. Someone with a grudge maybe?"

"You mean like you?" She smirked.

"Yes. If I wasn't me, I might put myself under suspicion."

"No one else has suggested it. You're supposed to be our knight in shining armor."

"So I can get away with anything?"

"You'd have to come back first to get away with anything."

Jep's chair squeaked as he leaned back and rocked for a moment. "I'll have to think about it."

"I was hoping you'd just say yes."

"I want to."

"What's stopping you?"

"Wisdom."

"It's hard to argue with that. But don't think too long, okay? We need you back there. Even if some people don't recognize it, the important ones do. And you said you trust my judgement, right?"

"Did I say that?" Jep grinned.

"It's why you still want me for a partner."

"Right."

"So you have to believe me."

"I'm more worried *you* don't trust *me*."

"I do. But while you ponder your next step, I should get back."

"I'll walk you out."

Jep gave Slate a look when they passed him, and he waggled his eyebrows.

"Thanks for letting me borrow him," she said to Slate.

"You can borrow him anytime. In fact—"

"That's enough," Jep said, putting a hand on Em's back to hurry her to the door. "There's no telling what would come out of his mouth," he whispered to Em. He'd worked hard to remove the crude from Slate's conversation, but the young man would never pass up an opportunity like this one.

"He seems like a handful," she said once they were outside.

"He can be, but he's a good kid."

She held out her hand to shake his. It was an awkward gesture that suggested she was stalling for time.

"So, uh…," she said, fidgeting with her purse strap. "If you come back, does that mean this place goes on pause?"

"No. I've got others who can help run it."

"I think it's really good what you're doing."

"Thank you. I'm not always so sure, but it's the only option I have, so I try to make the most of it."

"Not the only option."

"You know what I mean."

"Yeah. So…I guess I'll see you. I hope."

"I'll let you know."

Jep waved as she pulled out of the parking lot. Her visit raised a lot of questions. Most of those questions involved terrorists, but some personal ones muddied the water, and now was not the time to unravel them.

Chapter 12

EM HAD HELPED COLLATE the data recovered from the blast sight, so when Lawson called a briefing of the entire staff, she guessed what it was about.

"As you are by now aware, after we cross-referenced the names of those we've identified as well as bits of intel from various sites, we've pieced together what we believe may be the group's next target. Obviously, after what happened last time, we're being more cautious."

The elevator dinged and opened, and Em looked over to see Jep step off. She rubbed her hand across her mouth to keep from beaming, then glanced at Pearce, who had noticed his arrival too.

"Welcome back," Lawson said to Jep when he joined the group.

"Thank you, sir. It's good to be back."

"I trust you had a good break?"

So that's how they were going to play it. Pretend like nothing happened.

"It served its purpose."

Jep

Despite the scowl on Lawson's face, he said, "Jep will take the lead on this op once he's been fully briefed. As for the evidence—we now know that there is something planned for a park downtown. Jep, you've seen the summary. Do you have any initial thoughts?"

"A couple." He looked at Em. "But Emery knows more. I'd be curious to hear what she has to say."

Her face heated. "I, uh..." Her mind went blank. "Well, the data that we have. And the evidence—" She looked at Lawson, whose face was pinched in a confused glower. "—is timely. We should consider it carefully." She looked back at Jep. His eyebrows were lifted, and all she could do was shrug.

"Right," Lawson said. "Agent Booth, you can come to my office to go over the situation in detail. Then we'll regroup and get you guys out there on the street. Let's see if we can hunt these guys down and make them pay."

"What was that all about?" Pearce whispered to Em as everyone dispersed. "Was he trying to get back at you for something?"

"No, he thought I'd have valuable content to contribute." She slumped. "He was obviously wrong."

"You were unprepared. That's all. Happens to the best of us."

"I have never seen that happen before in this office. If I'd known he was going to do that—"

"He shouldn't have asked for your input anyway. It's not your job to speak about the details of an operation."

She deflated further. "No. I guess not. I was relieved

to see Lawson's approval of Jep's return. Or, at least, that's how it appeared."

Pearce looked toward Lawson's office. "Yeah. For now. But it's a thin thread. Jep might not feel it, but he's got a leash, and it doesn't stretch as far as it did."

"Don't say that. Jep's not stupid. He'll pick up on it."

"Lawson's not stupid either. He'll be careful."

"I wish they could stand on the common ground they have instead of…whatever it is that's going on."

"We'll have to wait and see how much self-control they both have."

"Do you know what happened between them?"

"Only what everyone else knows. An operation Jep was running went bad. People died. Booth says more people would have died if he'd done it Lawson's way. Lawson says the opposite."

"Who's right?"

"I wasn't part of the mission."

"You haven't looked at the file?"

"It wasn't my place. It's not your place either."

"But what if Lawson's the one in the wrong?"

"Jep's the one who left. I think that answers that question."

"No, it doesn't. He left of his own free will."

"What are you trying to say? You think Lawson's the bad guy here?"

"All I'm saying is I believe Jep's gotten a bad rap. I don't think he's the man everyone's made him out to be."

"I've never been against Jep, remember? I'm the one

Jep

who brought him in. But whatever happened on that mission, the bottom line is, he's not a guy who plays by the rules. You can't deny that's true. So, as much as I'm all for him being here, I'm also worried and determined to keep an eye on him. And you, since you're stuck with him."

"You ever think that maybe some of the rules need to be changed?"

"I can't believe I'm hearing this from you. You never struck me as the kind of person who would encourage rule breaking."

"I never said I encourage it."

"Don't get lost in this, Em. You're a good person, and I can understand why you want to stick up for someone who appears to be the underdog. But Jep can take care of himself. If you get too involved, you'll end up getting hurt."

She huffed in exasperation. "I keep telling everyone it's not Jep's fault that I got cut."

"That's not what I'm talking about." He moved closer. "You like your job, right?"

"Yeah."

"I'd hate for you to lose it on account of a guy like that."

"How could that happen?"

"Just don't let him drag you too deep, okay? I can't force you to change your mind about remaining his partner, but I want to know you'll be safe. Don't let your personal feelings get in the way."

"What personal feelings?"

His lips pressed together. "Any."

"There's nothing going on between us if that's what you're implying."

"I didn't say there was."

"And there won't be. Ever."

"Good."

"I have my head screwed on. My purpose in all of this is the same as everyone, to find out who's responsible for these deaths."

"Okay then, I'll leave you to it."

"Have a seat," Lawson said to Jep, his own chair squeaking as he leaned back.

"I'm okay to stand, thanks."

"Suit yourself. As I'm sure you've discovered, you have some weight to bandy around, but I warn you, it isn't much. I will concede that you have your strengths, and if I have to sacrifice a bit of pride to get the job done, then so be it. But one more mistake and you're finished, do you understand?"

"Can you define 'mistake'?"

Lawson splayed his fingers on the desk and studied them for a moment. "I've already lost too many good men and women. I expect you to put the safety of our people ahead of any personal ambition or drive."

"I always have, no matter what you think."

"As long as I have your word."

"You do."

"Once you know your course of action on this, I want you to give me the full picture before we bring it to the team. And I hope you will do me the courtesy of listening to any advice I have to offer."

"I can do that."

"Good. Then my first piece of advice is that you should choose Pearce as your new partner."

"Emery has said she'd like to continue."

Lawson tipped his head back. "Not this again. Jep, this is a dangerous game we're playing here. You say preserving life is high on your list, but you're talking about sending an analyst into the fire. It's irresponsible at best, and if anything were to happen to her, I'd call that murder."

"I get it. You still blame me for Agent Taggart's death. But you can't tell me you weren't letting your emotions interfere with the team on that assignment. I've never spoken to anyone about it, but I can't work under you when you insist on preserving illusions."

"I don't know what you're talking about."

"I know about the affair you were having with her."

"That's ridiculous."

"She told me. And it was her decision to go into the building that night, not mine."

"You were leading the op. You made changes without my authorization and against my better judgement."

"But your judgement wasn't better, was it? You were trying to protect Taggart, and she knew it. We all knew it. In the end, saving her life would have cost many others theirs."

Lawson's lips trembled, and his next words came out

dripping with venom. "And you were happy to send her to her death."

"I already told you she went against my orders. I was working on another plan."

"She wouldn't have done that."

"Yes she would, and you know it. She was a great agent. She often risked her life to get the job done."

"Say what you will. But if another one of my team dies on your watch, I'm holding you personally responsible."

Jep shifted to release some of the growing tension. "I have no intention of letting Em anywhere near danger."

"Are you saying that was your intention last time?"

"We weren't on a mission at the time. Things got out of hand."

"And you can swear to me that it won't happen again?"

"I swear. Is that all?"

"No. I want an explanation."

"Of what?"

"Why choose her anyway? If you're here for the good of the team, why insist on bringing her along on a mission? Because from where I'm sitting, it looks like a move whose sole purpose is to antagonize me."

"It has nothing to do with you. I'm here because your team needed fresh eyes. You needed someone who can look at this investigation from a different angle. Em helps me to do that. She's good. She sees details others miss."

"That's why she's an analyst."

"You could use her for a lot more."

Jep

Lawson pushed a file across the desk. "That's everything we have so far. Get back to me when you're finished."

Jep took the file. Lawson would continue to question his every move. "Thank you, sir."

When he left the room, Pearce was waiting for him.

"Welcome back."

"Thanks," Jep said but continued toward his desk.

"If you have any questions about any of the other agents—their strengths and weaknesses, you let me know. They've given us the best of the best."

"I'm sure they have."

Pearce put a hand on him to stop him. "I think on this op, you should consider hanging back. I know you won't let Em get too close, but I think we'd all do better if you gave your orders from the sideline."

"Why?"

"In case anything happens. We can't afford to lose you."

"But you can afford to lose the best of the best?"

"You know what I mean."

"I'll call it like I think it should go. And I have never once remained behind expecting my team to be the ones to put their lives in danger."

"I understand."

"Good."

"One more thing," Pearce said.

"Yes?"

"Em said she's staying on as your partner."

"I'll make sure she's safe."

"It's not that. I'm just curious why you chose her."

"Isn't everyone?"

"As a matter of fact, yes."

"If you don't know, I don't really have an answer for you."

"Then I hope it's for her skills. She's one of the good ones. Incorruptible, if you know what I mean."

"You're worried I'll take advantage of her?"

"I'm trying not to make assumptions about you, Booth, but I don't know you well, and Em needs looking out for. She's out of her depth, but I'm not sure she understands just how much."

"I think she understands more than you give her credit for."

"I hope so. But I want to make sure she's safe in all possible meanings of the word."

"She is." Jep slapped his arm. "I've got some reading to do, if you'll excuse me."

Chapter 13

"OKAY, TEAM." Jep clapped his hands to get their attention. "The information we have suggests an attack of some kind. However, we can't rule out the possibility that our foe has left that information for us to find. They could be waiting for us."

"Does that mean we don't make a move?" one of the agents said.

"No, it means we're going to be cautious and invisible. We can't ignore what we found. There are too many lives at stake. But if they left it for us to find, and we know that ahead of time, that means, for the first time, we're ahead of the game. We know something they don't. That's where the invisible part comes in. We're all going into the park in plain clothes. If they're expecting a team of agents, we don't want them to know that's what they've got. Pearce. You'll lead the second team into the park five minutes after the first."

"I thought I'd be in the tactical van."

"No, you're too experienced to stay behind on this. I

need you on the ground. You've had the most experience with our enemy as well as what they might be expecting from us, so I'm counting on you to be on top of this. "

"Yes, sir."

"If they're looking for us, we need to find them first and anything they've set up that's going to cause casualties or other damage. We all have to be thinking outside the box here. Middle Eastern terrorist groups have taken responsibility for the past events, but we haven't confirmed their involvement. That means no one is ruled out. Do you understand?" He waited for the group to acknowledge before he continued. "Because we don't know what type of environment we're walking into here, I expect anyone who sees suspicious activity to touch base with me first. Do not engage until I give the go ahead. You contact me over the radio, and we'll assess the threat. Unless, of course, the situation is critical."

Another agent spoke. "What is the best-case scenario here?"

"Best case is that we identify and extract at least one player without the others finding out. I realize that's a big ask, but if we can bring someone in without the others knowing, that will put us on a whole new playing field, which is exactly what we need."

"And if we can't?" Pearce said.

"If we can't, I'd settle for bringing in a suspect whatever way we can. I know the last time you had that opportunity, you weren't able to bring anyone back alive. I'm hoping things won't end so bloody this time around.

We need this." Comments of agreement filled the spaces around the room. "If everyone's ready, we'll move out."

Em followed Jep to his vehicle. "You look nice in jeans," he said, his gaze lingering.

"I learned my lesson. Don't worry," Em said, looking at the other two agents who were joining them as part of the initial team entering the park. "I want it noted by everyone in attendance here that, the last time we went out, Jep did not inform me I'd be approaching a prostitute."

The agents looked at each other and got in the car. Jep caught their dismay. They were right. He and Em were flirting, and it wasn't appropriate.

"Agent Bailey, Cramer, you two good?" he said to the men as he turned over the engine.

They buckled their seatbelts. "Ready when you are," Cramer said.

Jep drove past the park, then pulled over several blocks away to give them space to enter on foot. The tactical van was in place closer to the park.

"It's quieter than I expected," Cramer said as he got out of the car. "I thought they would have picked somewhere with more people."

"If the park was busy, it would be harder for them to spot us, right?" Em said. "This way, we'll be obvious. Even in plain clothes."

"That's a good point," Jep said. "It's easier to be invisible in a large crowd. We'll have to break up the groups further. I'll take Em in first to get a look around. It will be easy for us to blend in as a couple. Cramer. Bailey. I want you to approach separately." He spotted a food truck across the road. "Bailey, get some lunch and have it in the park. Cramer, make a phone call as you get close." He radioed to Pearce next.

"We're in position," Pearce said.

"Good, but there's been a slight change of plan. I need you guys to strengthen your cover. The park's too empty. We'll need to spread out our approach."

"Copy that."

"Make sure each of your guys has a good reason for being there."

"We do. Catching bad guys."

"Funny. We can't have anyone blowing our cover on this."

"Copy that. We'll give ourselves more backstory."

"Good. Emery and I are heading in first. Give us ten to fifteen minutes, then approach unless you hear from me. And only talk into the earpiece if absolutely necessary." He looked at Bailey and Cramer to make sure they were listening.

"We got it," Cramer said.

Jep put his radio away. "Actually, Cramer, hang on. I've got an idea." He went to the trunk of the car and pulled out a pair of binoculars. "Take these."

"You want me to hang back? Observe from a secluded location?"

"Nope. You've been promoted to a bird watcher. I want someone covering the wooded area toward the back of the park in case we get a runner."

Jep

"Bird watcher it is," Cramer said. "I bet there's an app for that." He pulled out his phone.

"All right," Jep said. "Let's do this."

He took Em's hand and drew her down the sidewalk.

"You think they're waiting for us?" Em whispered.

He looked at her with a grin. "We're not in earshot yet. You don't have to whisper."

"Oh, yeah? What about that guy?" She nodded behind her to the jogger that had run past.

"You think they have scouts? Did he do something to rouse your suspicion?"

"Not him. I was making a point. They could have eyes everywhere."

"Then we better sell it." He swung their hands. "That's better."

"We're going to be *that* kind of couple?"

"The cornier the better."

"Even acting like this, is hard to settle my nerves, and we're not even in the danger zone yet. Do you think they're waiting for us?"

"Not you. You're the only one of us that won't stand out."

"What do you mean? You've never looked like an agent." She shook her head and laughed.

"What?"

"When I first met you, I was so unimpressed with the way you dressed. I had no idea how much sense it all made."

"It comes with experience. You scared?"

"Not scared, but it's difficult to think clearly through the haze of tension."

"You say the word, and you can go back to the car."

"No. I want to do this. But how do you compartmentalize?"

"The nerves?"

"Any of it. How do you keep your emotions in check?"

He looked at her. He had emotions connected to her being on this job that he hadn't yet pushed behind a wall. He took a breath, making it happen now.

"Training," he said. "That's why Lawson didn't want you out in the field. You don't have the training to prepare you for what could happen. That's why I'm keeping you on the sidelines."

"Then why am I the first to go in?"

"That's when there's the least risk. You go in first and have a look around, then the rest of us come in when you're at a safe distance. Hopefully it won't matter. It could be that their plan isn't to attack yet. They had one big one recently. They may be doing this to gather more intel on our responses like they have in the past. Another good reason to go unnoticed. We don't want them getting what they're after."

"Either way, they won't be unprepared for us."

"And that's why you're going to stay at the edge of the park. Don't go near anyone, no matter how harmless they appear."

"It won't be easy watching you guys put yourselves in harm's way while I sit safe and secure."

Jep

"If anything dangerous happens, I don't expect you to watch. I expect you to run. Got it?"

"Yeah."

"Good. I saw a bench on the west side as we drove past. No one was near it. If anyone does approach you, you get up and get out of there."

"And if they don't?"

"Sit and scan. If you see anything suspicious, you tell me. I'll check it out."

"What if it's a mom with a baby?"

"That's suspicious?"

"No, I mean, what if a mom with a baby comes over to sit on the bench?"

"Then you politely excuse yourself as quickly as you can without drawing attention. I don't care who it is. I'm not taking any more chances with you."

"I should be grateful."

"Aren't you?"

"I guess I wish I could do more."

"You're already doing a lot, trust me. I forgot to ask you how that gun feels."

"I've had weapons training," she said.

"That's not what I asked."

"It feels odd because I'm not used to it, but it's also nice to know I can protect myself if I need to."

They continued down the sidewalk as they entered the area of the park, and Jep pulled her closer, putting an arm around her. He felt her arm curl around his waist, but it was tentative.

"You going to be okay?" he said. "Remember what I said. You can return to the car at any time."

"I don't want to let you guys down."

"You wouldn't. You want to go back?"

"No. Not yet." She looked around. "And now that we're here, my anxiety is easing a bit."

"Good. Anything stand out?"

"Nothing yet."

"That's the bench over there." He steered her down a path. "We'll sit down for minute together, then I'll go have a look around— Hang on." He bent down to pick up a candy wrapper that was wedged into the edge of the sidewalk.

"What's that for?"

"I need a reason to look in the garbage can."

"What about the other bins?" she said as he threw the wrapper away and peered inside at the collection of garbage. It appeared undisturbed.

"It's a clean park," he said. "But there's always trash. I'm sure I'll find enough if I look. Cigarette butts are always in abundance."

When they reached the bench, they both sat, and Jep reached his arm around behind Em, who leaned into his shoulder. "I can't see much from here," she said.

"You won't be the only one looking. Our bird watcher is on his way in now, and Bailey won't be far behind with his lunch."

"Still, I could see better from that rise over there."

"That's too deep into the park. There's not a clear exit from that position except for the wooded area, and I don't want you going that way."

"But Cramer will be covering it."

"I said no."

She huffed. "What if you escort me over? I'll have a look around for a few minutes, get a good look, then I'll head back here."

"Too risky. And I need you to cover this area."

She was quiet for a minute as she continued to scan the area. "I thought you chose me because I could see things others couldn't."

"I did."

"Then why aren't you using me to my full potential?"

"I am."

"No you're not. If I can't get a better view, there's no point in me being here. I only have part of the picture. I need more. I know you're a little gun shy after what happened last time, but it will be okay. I won't stay long. I just want to get a view of everything."

"I don't like it."

"I know. Tuck your emotions behind your training, and you'll be fine." She gave him a patronizing pat on the chest and stood. "Coming?"

"This has nothing to do with emotions." At least he would never admit that it did.

"One look."

"One short look, and you'll leave it alone? You'll come back here and sit for the duration without any more requests."

"Unless things get ugly, and then I will run as fast as I can away from here."

"Promise?"

"Yes."

He caught sight of Bailey biting into a hotdog as he

walked into the park. Cramer was already past the rise, and Pearce's team would be entering soon from the other side of the park. More eyes would be good, but he was beginning to regret bringing Em. She was a good asset to have on the team, but her presence made him jumpy.

He stood and took her hand but made her drag him for the first several steps. "You're a lot more work than I expected."

She grinned, pulling him forward. "I'll take that as a compliment."

He continued to resist, forcing her to slow down. "If we're doing this," he said. "Then we're going to make it count. Pay attention to everything."

"I am, but I was also thinking."

"About what?"

"You're leaving me at the bench when we get back, right?"

"Yes."

"What's your motivation? You wouldn't leave your girlfriend on her own at the park when we're on a date. Maybe I should slap you. Give you a reason for your actions."

"You need a slap to sell it?"

"Oh, absolutely."

He laughed freely as they reached the top of the rise, telling himself it was all for show. Then he put an arm over her shoulder and gave her a squeeze. "Whatever you think is necessary."

"It will have to be a hard one."

"Why?"

Jep

"It won't work if there's no red handprint."

"You're enjoying this too much. What happened to your nerves?"

"I'm hiding them behind amusement."

"Well, you had better be paying attention too. I won't bring you up here a second time."

"I haven't stopped my inspection. But we have to maintain our cover. I wonder what we're talking about right now that makes me angry enough to drive you away." Her eyes swept across the grounds as they bantered.

Jep kept a steady lookout. He wouldn't make the same mistake he made with the homeless guy. In here, everyone was a possible threat.

"Maybe I've told you I want to see other people," he said.

"No, that's no good. Anyone looking at us knows you're lucky to have me."

"Is that so?"

"It would make more sense that you're smothering me. I think I need space."

"I don't know. Your arm's holding me pretty tight."

He hadn't seen Pearce enter the park yet, but when his look passed Bailey, the other agent was looking at him.

"Slow down," Jep whispered as he watched the agent give him a barely perceptible nod before looking north.

Jep slowly turned his head and saw a man and a woman in bulky overcoats. It was cool outside, but not cold.

"Em, can you do me a favor?"

"What's that?"

"I want you to go back to the car. Forget the bench. Forget the slap. Move like you forgot something and wait for me there."

"What have you seen?"

"Stay calm. We're still in character."

"Where?" She tensed when she spotted the two figures.

Jep pulled at her. "Stop looking that way." He tugged her around so they were walking back the way they'd come. "Go to the car. Now."

"Wait—" She craned to look again, but he yanked her around and pulled her into him, brushing his mouth close to her ear.

"You can't look at them," he whispered. "We can't alert them to anything."

"I know, but—"

"No. I don't have time to argue. And whatever you do, don't turn that way again. Walk to the exit as casually as you can and wait at the car. Nod if you understand."

She nodded, and he kissed her cheek to keep up the ruse. He couldn't let them get wind of anything before Em was clear.

His hand dropped slowly from hers, as though he was reluctant to let her go. "I'll see you soon."

He turned, tucking his hands into his pockets as he made his way toward Bailey until he was out of the suspects' line of sight. Then he contacted his team.

"Pearce, are you in the park yet?"

Jep

"Almost there," Pearce said.

"We have a code orange, but don't rush. I think we're still incognito. Emery is on her way out of the park. We won't make a move till she's clear, so hold—" He cast a glance over his shoulder to check her progress but saw she was hurrying toward the two suspects. "What is she doing— Be advised we now have a code red. I repeat, code red. We have a friendly in imminent danger. Emery is twenty yards from the suspects and closing. I'm going in."

He darted sideways to remain out of the vision of the suspects. He signaled toward Bailey and Cramer, who moved into position until Jep spotted a couple who'd been having a picnic on a blanket. They'd jumped to their feet.

"Bailey, Cramer," Jep said into his earpiece. "You've got hostiles on your six. Pearce, we need backup now!"

Pearce came running with his team as Bailey and Cramer turned to face their attackers. Everyone was armed.

Jep sprinted toward the overcoats, focusing on Emery, who had the full attention of the two she was approaching at a jog.

The female suspect had her hand out as if to stop Emery from coming closer, while her other hand held her coat closed.

He could hear the shouts of "FBI" from his team, then shots were fired, and Em dropped to the ground.

Chapter 14

JEP HAD his weapon out as he picked up speed to reach Emery, trying to figure where the shots had come from and whether or not she had been hit.

"FBI!" he shouted when he was close enough. "Don't move. Put your hands in the air." The man in the overcoat pulled a gun, but before Jep could fire, another weapon discharged, and the man fell.

He looked for who fired and saw Em sitting up, still pointing her gun while the other suspect had her hands in the air and was staring wide-eyed at her dead companion. Jep rushed in before she could react.

"Keep your hands in the air," he shouted, noticing the bomb that was strapped to her chest. "Don't move. Em, you okay?" He couldn't see any blood on her. That was a good sign, but she didn't respond "Em! Have you been shot?" He kept looking between her and the woman, trying to secure the scene. Em still wasn't responding to him, but slowly, her arm lowered.

He moved in closer, keeping his aim on the woman,

and checked the man to confirm he was dead. He looked like he might be from the Middle East, but this woman did not, and there was something familiar about her.

"Where's the trigger for the bomb?" he said to the woman.

"In-in my pocket. It's not live." She looked at Emery.

"Don't worry about her," Jep said. "You focus on me. I'm the one you should be worried about. Not her."

"We weren't going to blow anything up."

"No offense, but I'm not taking your word for it."

The woman looked at Emery again, and Jep grunted.

"Hey," he said. "I'll tell you what. How about you keep your eyes on the ground?"

Reluctantly, the woman dropped her head and focused on the grass at her knees.

Jep tried Emery again. "Em?"

She was still focused on the dead man, but her eyes shifted to him when he spoke.

He smiled. "How're you doing?" She just blinked. "Everything will be okay, but can you do something for me?" She nodded slowly. "I need you to go to the car. Can you do that?"

She turned to the woman and shook her head.

"Em," he said sharply. "It's not safe here."

"I killed him," Em said to the woman.

The woman looked at her and frowned but nodded, then said, "Why are you here?"

"Hey," Jep snapped in her direction. "Don't talk to her."

The woman looked back at the ground.

He wasn't getting anywhere with either of them. If Em was in too much shock to cooperate, he'd have to secure the bomb with her still in the vicinity and make sure to keep her from having a heart-to-heart with the suspect.

"Which pocket is the trigger in?" he said to the woman.

"Left."

"Mine or yours."

"M-mine."

"You sure?"

"Yes."

"Emery." Jep kept his weapon trained on the suspect but moved to Em and grabbed her arm, tugging her back. "I need you to give us some space. Can you do that for me?"

She scooted a little, but not far. It was clear she was struggling to make sense of her surroundings. "You're in shock, okay? But I need you to listen to my voice—"

Pearce ran up. "We've got the area secure with—whoa. That's not good."

"She said it's not live."

"Course she did. What else is she going to say until she has the trigger in her hand? Why is Emery still here?"

"She's in shock."

Pearce lowered his voice so only Jep could hear. "We

Jep

should eliminate the threat. One shot, and we're all safe."

"That's out of the question."

"She killed our own. Agents we both knew and respected. We'd be within our rights to do so."

"*She* didn't do it. And the only way we'll find out who's responsible is if we have a suspect to question. Where are we at with the others?"

"Deceased. This guy makes three."

"So she's all we've got."

"Yeah." He straightened. "We've got more agents on the way, and the bomb squad is on standby. I'll let them know they're needed."

He stepped away and radioed it in. Then Jep said, "Can I trust you to take over from here, Pearce? You understand we're taking the suspect in alive?"

"Yeah, of course. I was just making sure we'd considered all of our options."

"Good. I'll get Emery out of here."

"She's not looking too good." Pearce pulled his gun and aimed at the woman.

Jep returned his weapon to its holster. "Em's the one who shot that guy."

Pearce looked back at the dead man. "She did that?"

"Yeah."

"That was a good shot."

"She shouldn't have been here," the woman said.

"Excuse me?" Pearce said.

"Why is she here?" The look on her face passed between anger and fear.

"I don't think that's any of your business."

"She messed everything up."

"My apologies for the inconvenience. Next time, we'll do things your way. Or how about this? How about you lost your rights when you strapped a bomb to your chest?"

"I already told the other guy, it's not live."

"Save it for the interrogation," Jep said as he knelt beside Emery.

"She couldn't have known I was here," the woman said.

"I think you might be out of your mind," Pearce said. "I hate to break it to you, but the insanity plea doesn't work when it comes to terrorism because, at heart, you're all a bunch of lunatics already."

Em was rolling a piece of grass between her fingers as Jep leaned closer.

"You mind if I take this?" he said gently as he lifted her hand, which still held the gun.

Em looked up at him when he spoke, like she'd only just realized he was there.

"You saved my life, you know," he said after he pried the weapon from her hand and tucked it into the back of his pants. "That was very brave."

She mumbled something, then looked back at the woman.

"Em? Talk to me." He took her arm when she didn't respond. "Why didn't you go back to the car when I asked you to?"

She focused back on him again. "I couldn't leave her."

"Who? That woman?"

Jep

"You would have killed her. Or she would have killed you. Either way...I couldn't...I had to do something, but then...that man had a gun."

"Is this because of the prostitute from the other day? I know I told you we could try to help her, but this was different. Today, the woman needed to be stopped before she could have help."

Em's breathing sped up with her agitation. "No, I couldn't let you—" Tears appeared in her eyes.

"Why did you have to protect her?"

"Because she's my sister."

Jep glanced at the woman and let out a long, slow breath. He now understood what about the woman had looked familiar. It was the family resemblance.

A hand rested on his shoulder. The man standing above Jep was wearing full protective gear. "We're going to need you to clear out while we deal with this."

The bomb squad had arrived.

"Yeah. Give us a second." He shook his head to reset. "Okay, Em. We can talk about that, but we're going to have to move while we do." He lifted her, checking to make sure her legs would hold before he led her away, but she resisted. "They'll take good care of her," he said. "But we've got to get out of blast— We have to get out of the way before they can do that."

"They won't hurt her?" Em said, her eyes round as a kitten. Innocent and searching.

"No."

"How do you know?"

"Because that's the order I gave."

"What if they don't listen?"

"They will."

"How can you be sure?"

Jep put his arm around her, forcing her to take the first few steps. He'd carry her away if he had to, but once they got moving, she walked on her own.

"We all want to bring her in uninjured," he said. "We need to question her. She's safe."

"There's no way she knew what she was doing."

"She had a bomb strapped to her."

"No. She would never hurt anyone."

"Don't worry about any of that right now, okay? She'll have the chance to explain herself."

"Okay."

He led her down the hill to the sidewalk, past a crowd of agents and police.

An officer lifted the barricade tape so they could duck under, and Jep waited until they were far enough away that they had some privacy before asking her any questions. He'd have to be careful how he worded them.

"Were there any signs that your sister had extremist connections? Did she have a boyfriend who might have been involved?"

Em shook her head. "I have no idea—" She looked at Jep in horror. "Do you think that was her boyfriend who I killed?"

"No. I saw no indication of that." Was it a lie if he genuinely didn't know?

She gripped his arm tighter. "I can't make sense of this."

"Do you know if she was hanging out in any night clubs or bars or anywhere?"

Jep

"Last I knew, she was overseas."

"Did she tell you that?"

"She sends postcards to my aunt while she's traveling."

"What about phone calls? When's the last time you spoke to her?"

"Not in a long time. We don't really talk. We haven't been close since…"

"Since when?"

"Since, ever. Even as kids, we didn't play much. She was always busy doing her own thing. All I know is she's been traveling the world for a while."

"Do you know if your aunt saved the postcard?"

"Yeah, she— Who are they?"

Jep saw the group crossing the road and gritted his teeth. "Reporters."

"They'll get a picture of my sister. She'll be all over the news. I have to call Carla. She can't find out that way."

"No. You can't tell anyone."

"But she'll see Jade on the news."

"No she won't. We need to keep this confidential. We won't let anyone know who we have in custody. Don't worry."

"You're sure?"

"It's not the first time we've done it." Em tripped, but Jep caught her. "Whoa. Let's slow down. We don't need to be in a rush to get anywhere."

"I can't believe this is happening. She's gotten herself into trouble before, but not like this. Never like this."

"People who are searching for purpose sometimes find it in the worst places."

"But she's not looking for purpose. All she's ever cared about is her own self-gratification. She looks out for number one and no one else. Why would she suddenly be okay with murder?"

"People change."

"You say that like it's a normal life choice to kill people."

"I don't mean to diminish what's happening to your sister. We won't know what's really going on until we speak to her."

"I don't know what I'm going to do."

"You don't have to do anything besides decompress. And the agency has people you can talk to."

"The only person I want to talk to is my sister, but they won't let me see her, will they? It's personal, so I won't be assigned to the file. I know how this works."

"Probably not, but you never know. Stranger things have happened."

"What if she won't speak to anyone? What if she says she'll only speak to me?"

"Do you think she will?"

"I have no idea, but will they let me see her if she does?"

"Each case is different. We won't know until it happens." He paused. "You know they'll question you too, right? You need to be prepared for that."

"But I don't know anything. What do they expect me to say?"

"Everything you just told me. You said her name is Jade?"

"I don't think I can do this."

"You can. I know you can. You're stronger than you think. It feels overwhelming right now, but it's all really fresh. It will ease off soon."

"Can you be the one to question me? Will they let you?"

"They don't usually let partners question each other."

"Then I won't be your partner anymore."

"Is that what you want?"

"No."

She shook her head and curled her arms against her chest.

"Let me take you home. You need time to recover."

She didn't resist as he helped her into the car.

Chapter 15

"YOU COMING?" Jep said after they reached Em's apartment building when she didn't get out of the car.

She'd been so focused on her sister, she'd forgotten for a moment about the man she'd killed. The reality of what she'd done washed over her again.

When the shooting had started, all she had thought to do was drop to the ground and cover her head. But then that man had pulled his gun, and Jep was there. She couldn't even remember taking the weapon out of the holster. But she remembered pulling the trigger.

She'd killed a man, and her sister was a terrorist, prepared to blow herself up in order to kill innocent people. Her life had spun into chaos in seconds.

"Em?"

She swallowed. "Yeah, sorry." Her fingers fumbled with the door. When she finally climbed out onto the sidewalk, her legs wobbled, and she leaned against the car for support.

"Maybe this isn't the best place for you right now,"

Jep said, taking her arm to steady her as she attempted to stand again. "Are you going to be okay on your own? Is there somewhere else I can take you?"

She thought of her aunt, but Carla would fuss over her, and Em didn't think she could handle that when she wasn't allowed to share what had happened.

"I'll be fine." It wasn't true, but what other option did she have? Maybe space was what she needed to make sense of the crazy turn life had taken. Or maybe it would be the thing to pull her into a deeper pit of confusion and despair.

"I'll take you up," he said, leading her inside.

She could feel him watching her as the elevator rose but couldn't lift her eyes off the floor.

When the door opened, it took her a moment to get up the courage to step off. Then, at her door to her apartment, she struggled to get the key into the lock.

Jep rested his hand over her shaking one. "Let me do it." He slid her hand off the key and unlocked the door.

"I don't know what's wrong with me." She stumbled down the short hallway into the main living area.

"There's nothing wrong with you. Your reaction is perfectly natural."

"Oh yeah? Is this how you acted the first time you killed someone?"

"I grew up pretty rough," he said, tossing the keys on a small round dining table with a bowl of fruit in the middle of it. "I saw someone die when I was eleven. I was in a bad part of town, and a guy got knifed in the street."

"That's horrible."

"It shook me up bad. I didn't leave the house for a few days."

"No kid should—" The blood drain from her face, and her stomach turned. "I don't feel good."

"You don't look—" He caught her before she fell to the ground. "—so good."

The words were an echo as the blackness swallowed her.

As awareness returned, relief washed over her. She'd had a bad dream. A very bad dream. Maybe Carla was right. Maybe she hadn't fully forgiven her sister. Why else would she dream that her sister was a terrorist?

"Em?"

The male voice startled her. Where was she? At work?

"Em. You back with me?"

She blinked awake as pieces of the world slipped back into place, and an icy chill threatened to pull her back into the darkness. "It wasn't a dream," she whispered.

"You fainted."

"How long?"

"Long enough for me to lay you on the couch, but not more than that. I'll get you a drink of water."

He pushed himself up off his knees, but panic tightened in her chest.

"No." She shot up and grabbed hold of the sleeve of

Jep

his shirt, her fingernails stabbing into her palm through the soft fabric. The room spun again, and she laid back, pulling him with her.

"Hey, shh." Jep leaned closer, whispering into her hair. "It's going to be okay." The weight of his presence so close held her together as tears pricked at her eyes. His scent of mint and pine took her back to the first time they'd met. Before everything had capsized.

"I thought it was a dream," she said. "I was relieved. I wish I could have stayed asleep."

"I'm so sorry." The resonance of his voice purred through her body, easing the pins and needles.

"Why?"

"I shouldn't have brought you to the park." He leaned back so he could look at her, but he was still close enough that she could see the stubble beginning to show on his jaw. The fear slid away, but what took its place was alarming as well. The moment carried too much intensity, adding weight to an unspoken attraction between them. She needed to stop it. This couldn't happen. *They* couldn't happen.

"You need a shave," she said.

He let out a light, breathy laugh and rubbed his jaw as he leaned away to give her more distance.

"Yeah. Another reason for you to give me up as a partner. I'm too grubby."

"Maybe. But you're still the only one who believes in me."

"And where'd that get you? Look at you. You're falling apart, and that's my fault."

"You give yourself too much credit. And I'm feeling better." She *did* feel better. Stronger. So she pushed herself up to sitting. It helped diminish her sense of vulnerability.

"I'm not comfortable leaving you on your own like this," he said.

"I'll be okay. All I needed was time to settle in. But if you don't mind waiting, I could use another couple of minutes. To make sure. But I think the worst has passed."

She knew she couldn't keep him there forever, no matter how much she wanted to. He wasn't hers. He never would be, and she'd be okay with that. There was someone else God had for her. She wouldn't compromise on that. Not when her faith was such an integral part of her life. If her future husband couldn't share that part of who she was at her core, it would be too much to bear for a lifetime.

"You going to be okay if I get you that drink now?" Jep said.

"Yeah."

When he got up, he left a cold wall next to her. She knew when he returned, it would still be there. The moment had passed, and they'd both survived unscathed.

Jep fumbled through cupboards, opening every door that looked like it *wouldn't* have a cup just to make it take

Jep

longer. He had been a breath away from kissing her. It would have meant he'd taken advantage of her in her weakest moment. Maybe he was as bad as everyone thought. As bad as she'd thought he was from the start, and she didn't deserve that.

He took his time filling the glass once he'd found it, then brought it to her and sat in a chair across the coffee table.

"You sure you don't want to call your aunt before I go?" he said.

"No. I'll call her if I need to." She took a sip. "I don't want you to leave thinking you've done anything wrong," she said, and immediately he thought of the almost kiss. "Knowing that my sister was at the park," she continued. "Even after what happened, I'm glad I was there. Who knows what would have happened otherwise?"

His fingers rubbed on the arm of the chair while he battled what remained of his protective instinct for her. He wanted to be near her and hold her, whether she needed it or not.

"I should go," he blurted. Standing. "If you think you'll be okay."

"I'm much better. Thanks for everything. I'm glad you were here."

His lips flattened into a frown. "I wish today had gone differently." In more ways than he would ever admit. "Give me a call if you need anything. Even if you need to talk stuff through."

"I will."

Jep headed for the door when Em added, "Jep—"

He turned. "Just because something's hard doesn't mean it's wrong."

"What?" He couldn't find his breath.

"Everyone is worried about me. You think I shouldn't have been at the park because it was hard to take, but that doesn't mean it's wrong."

"Oh. Yeah."

"Don't let anyone tell you you shouldn't have brought me, okay? I'm tired of you all deciding what I can and can't handle."

Jep's phone buzzed, and he checked it. "It's from Pearce. They've got Jade in custody. I'll head in now and see how everything's going. Make sure they're treating her okay."

"They have every right to do what they please. If she's responsible for—" She squeezed her eyes shut for a moment. "I wouldn't blame them for being rough."

"That doesn't mean they should be. We have laws in this country about that."

"Do you know what kind of time she'll face if she's convic—*when* she's convicted."

"That depends on a lot of factors. If she cooperates and the information she gives us helps us apprehend whoever is leading this, that will work highly in her favor. Also, because she didn't pull a weapon on us, and she didn't have the trigger armed, they'll take all of that into consideration."

"Maybe she didn't want to do it. Maybe she was coerced somehow."

"Maybe."

Jep

"You don't think so?"

"We won't know until we talk to her. But whether or not she changed her mind in the end, she was there. She was part of it, and there wasn't a lot of remorse that I saw besides her frustration with you being present. She said it messed up their plans."

"I don't remember."

"You were pretty out of it."

"Make sure Lawson knows that. That it was because I was there that more people weren't hurt."

"I don't know he'll see it that way."

"He has to. If I hadn't been there, you could all be dead."

"Don't worry about Lawson. I can handle him. You rest, but call me if you need anything."

"I will. Thank you."

Jep went back to his car, frustrated by the sense of disappointment he carried with him. He had no doubt he'd done the right thing in stopping any kind of intimacy between them, but that didn't erase the feelings that lingered. She'd needed him there to comfort her while she was shaky, but that was it. It was her vulnerability that had presented the opportunity for more.

After starting the car, he sat and stared at nothing. He'd never let anything like this happen before. But he'd never felt anything like this before. He'd thought partnering with Em was a masterstroke at the start, but it had backfired on him in ways he never could have imagined. Lawson had been right, and he was prepared to take a hit to his pride and do what he was asked. He'd take Pearce on as a partner and finish the job. It was the perfect time for it. Em wouldn't be allowed close to the investigation anyway, not with her sister was in the picture.

With the decision made, he pulled into traffic, feeling a sense of relief that he could get himself back on track and finish the job he'd been brought here for.

Chapter 16

AFTER A FITFUL NIGHT'S SLEEP, Jep was grumpy and disheveled. Lawson had sent him on a pointless errand after he'd returned to the office, and the word was that Jade wasn't in a cooperating mood. Hopefully, with a little time locked up, that would change.

When he entered the office, he saw Emery at her desk, running her finger back and forth across the side of her temple. He went over to see her.

"Hey," he said.

She jumped. "Sorry, I was lost in thought."

"I didn't mean to scare you. You do okay last night?"

"Yeah. I slept pretty well, actually. Surprisingly."

"You didn't want to take time off? You can, you know. In fact, I'm surprised Lawson let you back into the office." He dragged a chair from a nearby desk and sat.

"All I got from him was a frown. Then he sent Pearce over."

"To do what?"

"Be the nice guy. Tell me I look tired, and I should go home for the rest of the week."

"It's not bad advice."

"Oh yeah? Go home and do what? Wander around my house? Stare at the wall as I endlessly pace? If the tables were turned, I'm sure you would jump at the opportunity."

"Good point. Work is better."

Em fidgeted with her pen. "Did you hear they're bringing my aunt in for questioning?"

"I did, yeah. Have you spoken to her? Do you know how she's taking it?"

"No idea. They didn't want me to have any contact with her."

"I'm not surprised."

"She's tough. She'll be okay, although I'd be surprised if she has anything helpful to add. Neither one of us knows much about Jade at all."

"You'd be surprised what one small piece of information can do. It could give us leverage to get Jade to open up."

"I hope they'll let Carla know what's going on so we can talk about it later."

"They'll give her as little as they can, but if she's smart, she'll piece it together."

"It wouldn't be the first time Jade's gotten herself stuck in a bad situation. But she's always weaseled her way out again."

"That won't happen this time."

"I know." She rubbed at her head again. "I hope she's smart and cooperates. I don't know why she wouldn't, but if she's really bought into these ideals, anything's possible."

He pointed toward her head. "Is that a headache? Or did you get hurt?"

She pulled her hand away and looked at her fingers. "I don't know I'm doing it half the time. It's 'cause I'm worried about Jade." She pushed her hair out of the way. "Old injury."

He had to lean in to see it. "Oh yeah. There it is. Little baby scar."

She shook her head in mock indignation. "It hurt when it happened."

"I hope the story is better than the damage."

"I was eight. Jade and I were playing at a creek down the road from where we lived. I slipped on the rocks and fell in. Bumped my head when I hit the water. It was the one time in my life my sister looked out for me."

"I doubt that's true. You probably just don't remember the others."

"The only person my sister has ever been interested in is herself. The only way I could even get her to come to the creek with me is if I promised to give her my dessert at dinner."

"Ouch. Your parents never noticed?"

"Are you kidding? Jade learned it from our mom. You never got anything for nothing with her either. I did all the laundry so she'd come to my room and say goodnight to me when I went to bed—I don't know why I'm telling you all of this."

"Sounds like you had it rough growing up."

"I shouldn't complain. I know others had it worse than I did. You saw a guy die when you were a kid."

"That doesn't lessen your pain. Was your dad around at all?"

"He was a very successful salesman for a pharmaceutical company, so he was away a lot."

"At least it put food on the table."

"This might sound weird, but it would have been better if he couldn't."

"That does sound weird."

"If my mom had *had* to work, maybe things would have been different. I don't know if she drank because she was bored or not, but I can't remember a time she wasn't off her face. If she had a job to go to, maybe it would have kept her sober."

"Where does your aunt fit into all of this?"

"After my dad left us, my mom…she didn't cope. Eventually it got so bad the neighbors called child services, and that's when Jade and I went to live with Carla. The saddest part was that I can't remember feeling sad. I was just relieved. For the first time in my life, I knew what it meant to have someone look after you."

"Then I'm glad you had your aunt. That's tough."

She shrugged. "It had a happy ending…until now."

"It could have been worse."

"I guess so. It's a hard argument to take hold of, though. It's like telling a kid to eat their vegetables because there are starving kids in Africa. What about you?"

"What *about* me?"

"What's your story? Did you know your parents?"

"You really want to go there?"

"It will help take my mind off everything."

"There's not much to tell."

"Yesterday you said you saw a man knifed in the street. That's a lot, and that's only one story."

"My life is pretty stock standard for a kid on the wrong side of the tracks."

"Yeah?" She leaned forward in interest, so Jep relented with a sigh.

"I never knew my dad," he said.

"Any siblings?"

"Probably should have, but no."

"Should have?"

"My mom was a prostitute. Loved me as best as she could, but...I spent most of the time looking after myself like you. If she ever got pregnant again, she took care of it before I knew anything about it."

"Oh."

"Don't feel sorry for me. I don't. It's like you said, we all have a hard story to tell. I've made peace with my past."

"Is that why you wanted to help that girl from the other day? Did she remind you of your mom?"

Jep shrugged. "I didn't even think about it that way, but maybe. That could explain my lapse in judgement."

"That wasn't a lapse in judgement. It was unforeseen."

"We'll agree to disagree."

"Just think about how much worse it could have been." Em's eyes shifted over his shoulder, and he turned to see a woman in her fifties approaching with a big smile on her face. She slid up to Jep with both her hands reaching for his.

He stood to greet her. "Good morning. You must be Carla."

"Hi there," she said, squeezing his fingers. "I am, indeed. And who might you be?"

"Don't mind her," Em said to Jep. "She's informal with everyone."

"Not a bad way to be," Jep said. "It's a pleasure to meet you. I'm Jep Booth."

Carla pressed her lips together and sent a quick look to Emery. "Is Jep short for something?"

"Jephthah."

"Hang on," Em said. "I didn't know that."

"You probably never asked," Carla said. "That's an unusual name, Jep."

"That's why I go with the shortened version. It's easier on everyone."

"What's the origin?"

"Hebrew, I think."

"Interesting. Was your mom religious?"

"No. Not at all. I have no idea what gave her the idea. Now, if you ladies will excuse me, Carla, I'll let the assistant director know you're here."

Carla twisted as she sat in the chair Jep had been using so she could watch him walk away. "*That's* Jep?"

"Don't."

"I didn't. I mean—I did. Oh my goodness. He is—" She fanned her face with her hand.

"Stop it."

"You're saying you're not attracted to him in the least?"

"I never said I wasn't attracted to him."

"Sure you did. After you first met him."

"I said a person's attractiveness changes as you get to know them better."

"Because you didn't think you would like him, but then you said—"

"I know what I said."

"I'm sorry. I shouldn't tease. The last thing I want is for you to get hurt."

"I won't. There's nothing going on."

"Nothing at all?"

"No."

"So you're going to ignore it until it goes away?"

"There's nothing to ignore. Why are we even talking about this? Aren't you concerned about why you're here?"

"I thought if it was something terrible, you would have told me already."

"They wouldn't let me speak to you."

Carla's smile faded. "Is it bad?"

"Miss Chapman?" Lawson had come out of his office, and both women looked up. "Sorry," he said as he walked to the desk. "Miss Carla Chapman." He shook her hand. "I'm Assistant Director Richard Lawson. Thank you for coming in so quickly."

"Didn't know I had a choice, but I'm happy to help

if I can." She looked at Em and stood slowly before turning back to Lawson. "My niece isn't in any trouble, is she?"

"Who, Emery? No, she's not in any trouble."

"Then what's this about?"

"If you'd like to come with me, I'll get you settled in one of our conference rooms. Can I get you anything to drink?"

"Em?" Carla said. A furrow had appeared on her brow. Em couldn't remember the last time she'd seen her aunt worried.

"It's okay," Em said. "Go ahead. He'll explain what he can. I'll get her a coffee, sir."

Carla clutched her purse to her stomach as Lawson led her away.

Em closed her eyes for a second to steady herself, then went to the kitchen, where Pearce found her.

"I was hoping to have a word with you," he said. "Wanted to make sure you were okay."

"I wish everyone would stop worrying about me so much." She focused on the cup as she added two sachets of sugar.

"We'd worry if it were any one of us. This is a big deal. Nothing has been normal for you since Jep turned up. Even Gardener's concerned, and she's not one for showing any kind of emotion."

"I think she's worried she's going to lose her mole. She likes having someone from her department out in the field." Em forced a smile. "We get to see firsthand what we usually only hear about when you guys finally come back to the office and write your reports."

"Em." He put a hand on her arm to get her to face him, but all she could do was grip the cup and stare into it. "After what happened yesterday, you must be ready for things to return to the way they were. You have enough disruption in your life right now. You don't need to add fuel to that fire."

"Nothing will make this any easier."

"You're upset. I don't blame you. Jep promised he'd keep you away from danger, and he sent you right into it. Again. And this time, you had the trauma not only of being forced to kill a man, but to see your sister like that—that's a lot for anyone."

Now she turned to him. "It was my idea to go up onto the rise, and I was the one who disobeyed an order and went to my sister. Besides which, if I hadn't been there, there's no telling who else could have died. I'm glad I was there."

"But it was Jep's responsibility to keep you safe."

"Can we change the subject?"

"He's a good agent, but I can't help but feel he has his own agenda."

Em refused to bite. "How're things going with Jade?"

"Okay, we don't have to talk about Jep."

"Good."

"I wish I had better news for you. Your sister's not talking."

"At all? Does she know that answering our questions will help her situation? Does she know how much trouble she's in?"

"Yes. We know how to interrogate a suspect—sorry,

I don't mean to— It's frustrating to be so close and yet continue to come up emptyhanded."

"What if I spoke to her?"

"I don't think Lawson would go for it. And I can't see how it would make any difference. You'd just be wasting your time."

"Then I'll waste my time. Or I'll get her to cooperate. We won't know unless we try."

"What about Lawson?"

"He's busy. "

"Emery Chapman circumventing protocol. So you *do* have it in you after all."

"Must be all this field work I'm doing. Getting a taste for it. Come on. A couple of minutes. If she didn't set off that bomb because of me, then maybe I have some influence with her."

Pearce looked out the kitchen door, then looked at his watch. "Okay, but you won't have long."

Chapter 17

"I DON'T SUPPOSE there's any chance you'll let me speak to her alone?" Em said when they reached the room where Jade was being held.

"No. Sorry. Getting you in here is as far across the line as I'll go, and it's only because I'm hoping it will make a difference."

He unlocked the door and entered the room with Emery right behind him.

Jade's head was dipped, but her eyes looked out from under her brow when they entered and tracked Em as she carefully pulled the chair out and sat.

Em looked back at Pearce—who was standing in the corner clasping his hands in front of him—and nodded.

It was hard to look her sister in the eye, but she managed. "Are you hungry or thirsty?" Em said.

The chain from Jade's cuffs rattled as she lifted her hands, pulled a chunk of blonde hair from her ponytail, and twisted it around her finger.

They didn't share much in the way of looks. Jade was much more their father. She had his strong jaw and striking green eyes. But they both had their mom's small, straight nose and blonde hair.

"I've already eaten," Jade said. "It's nice to see you, Emmy. You didn't look too good at the park."

"I'm sorry things are like this."

"Are you? I thought maybe you were enjoying yourself. You look smug."

"No, I don't."

"Did they send you in here cause they thought you'd get me to talk?"

"I was hoping I could help you."

"You got keys for my cuffs? That would help."

"I want to help you not get put away for the rest of your life."

"What difference does that make to you?"

"You're my sister."

"We'd see each other as often."

Jade had always been cool and collected. Her movements measured and precise. Even now, she kept her voice steady. But she carried a sadness in her eyes Em couldn't remember.

"What happened to you?" Em said.

"So many things. I've lived two lifetimes while you've been stuck in this stuffy building. Congratulations, by the way. I didn't know you'd gotten a job with the feds."

Jade was trying to put her on the back foot like she always did. Em had to get answers from her without letting it become personal.

"When did you get back to America?" Em said. "I thought you were in Cambodia."

"I was."

"Is that where you were convinced that killing innocent people was a good thing?"

"So you *are* here to get me to talk. Since when have I ever been swayed by you?"

"Never. But if you don't cooperate, I can't help you."

"You always did like to pretend you cared about me."

"You don't think I do? You're the one—"

"I think we're done here."

"You'll go to prison for a long time. Is that what you want?"

"Don't know. I've never been. Maybe I'd like it."

"If you tell us who you are working for—"

"—You're wasting your time."

"You don't want to help yourself?"

"Here we go again. The false concern."

"I've always cared about you."

"No. You've always been too busy showing off to whoever is most important in your life. First mom, then Carla, now who is it?" She looked at Pearce. "Him? You two having a little office romance?" She made a rude gesture with her hands.

"I'm not showing off. I'm trying to protect people. You and whoever your colleagues are trying to hurt."

"Do you still chew your fingernails?"

"Not since I was a teenager." Em held up her hand to show her sister. "It was connected to my anxiety, so when I learned to handle it better, I stopped."

"Just like that?"

"No. It took a lot of self-discipline."

"Well done. I'd clap for you, but…I couldn't be bothered, what with all this metal dangling off me."

"Why are you being like this?"

"Like what?"

"We were never close, but you didn't used to be rude and sarcastic."

"People change. Sorry to disappoint you."

"You act like none of this matters. That seeing me has no effect on you, but you didn't follow through on your plan in the park because I was there. You can't deny that."

"I'm not denying anything. I was in shock when I saw you. That's all. I thought maybe someone knew you were my sister and was playing a joke. Turns out it was a coincidence."

Em shook her head. "This isn't you. You're either lying, or they've messed with your head so bad—"

"Maybe it's because I'm being held here against my will. It doesn't garner the best of feelings. If you let me go, I'll be more friendly."

"You were prepared to kill people."

Jade glanced at Pearce. "I didn't do anything wrong. I never hurt anyone."

"But your intent was to do harm."

"How can you sit here in your pretty blouse and high-heeled shoes and act like you know anything of the world? You should never have come in here. I have nothing to give you. Why don't you go back to your lovely little life and forget all about me. You're good at that."

"You're the one who left."

"What choice did I have?"

"What's that supposed to mean?"

"There was nothing there for me," Jade said. "You had that all tied up for yourself."

"What are you talking about?"

"You had mom wrapped around your finger."

"I don't know how your memory is so skewed, but I had to do everything. The cooking, the cleaning—"

"Spare me. You loved every second of it. All you ever cared about was pleasing everyone. Everyone but me. Pretty little housemaker."

"I did all that because there was no one else to do it. Mom was passed out most of the time—"

"And that's why you were her favorite, because you let her shirk all her responsibilities. Then we went to Carla's, and you took her all for yourself too."

"You were never around. You didn't even give her a chance. And I wasn't anyone's favorite."

"Of course you were. You were the good-looking one, the smart one, the clever one. I was the screw up."

"That's why you left? Because you thought everyone liked me better? What I wanted the most was my big sister."

"Well, here I am. Now you get everything you want."

Em stared at her lap. This wasn't working. If she couldn't keep their personal baggage out of the way, it would be impossible to see through to the truth. "The bomb wasn't armed, but it could have been. Why didn't you blow us all up?"

"I should have. What can I say? It turns out I'm a big softy after all. Which means I'm useless to everyone." She glanced at Pearce again. "What a big surprise. But don't worry, sis. I won't let it happen again."

"You won't have the chance again. But you can still save more lives if you work with us."

"Listen to you. Let it go, will you? You're so self-righteous and ignorant."

"About what?"

"The world. You've stayed in your safe little bubble your whole life, while I've been out there seeing what it's really like. And you know what I've discovered?"

"What?"

"That the world isn't fair. People are suffering, and lo and behold, America can sometimes be the bad guy pulling the wings off of flies."

"Those agents that died in the last blast had family and friends. You think their kids aren't suffering right now?"

"Right along with the rest of the world. But real change requires sacrifice."

"Maybe if you had stayed with people you cared about, you would have seen some of the good there is."

"I had to leave my family to care about anything."

"All you're doing is making things worse. What happened to you that brought you to a place where you're willing to murder innocent people? When was it that you switched from having a great time traipsing the globe to strapping a bomb to your chest?"

Jade scoffed. "You really are thick, aren't you?"

"Then help me understand."

"You think I was having a good time?"

"That's what every postcard said."

"Have you ever noticed that it's usually the people who put up those obnoxiously happy posts on social media spewing garbage about how great their lives are that are the ones in the pit of despair? One second, they're married to the most amazing man on the planet, then the next they're getting divorced and shouting venomous accusations at their partner."

"If you were so miserable, you should have come home."

"And do what? Sit around in your shadow? Look at you in your silk blouse with your fancy job. At least I have purpose."

"Aunt Carla offered you purpose."

"What? You mean church?" Jade groaned. "That was the worst of all. I know you got sucked into all that airy fairy nonsense, but that wasn't for me."

"And this is?"

"Yeah. This is real. Are you willing to die for your beliefs? Are you willing to kill?"

It was an interesting question. Would she be willing to die for her faith? But she had to keep the focus on Jade.

"How long have you been back in the States?" Em said.

"Back to the statistics of my movements, huh? Did I cut a little too close to home? Don't want to get too deep now, do we? Sorry. I'd hate to make you uncomfortable."

"How long have you been back?"

"Not long."

"Where were you staying?"

Jade smiled. "No comment."

"More people could die."

"More people *will* die."

"When? Where?"

"Freedom comes at a price."

"Freedom from what? Law? Goodness?"

"This is becoming tedious."

"You can make it stop. All you have to do is tell me who you're working for."

Jade sighed dramatically. "No comment."

"I told you it would be a waste of time," Pearce said.

"Oh," Jade said. "It speaks. I thought maybe you'd turned into a statue."

"I can't help you if you don't talk to me," Em said.

"Then don't help me."

Em slammed her hand on the table. She was running out of time. "You're as selfish as you've always been. It's always about you. You never cared about anyone but yourself."

"Then I guess we're done here." Jade leaned back in the chair and closed her eyes.

"It doesn't have to be like this," Em mumbled but got up from her chair. "If you change your mind, I'll be around."

"Don't hold your breath."

Em quickly left the room before she could say

anymore. Anger, fear, and frustration were boiling up in her gut. She needed to find Jep. He'd understand her pain.

"Family's hard," Pearce said from behind.

"I really thought I could get through to her."

"I think it was like she said. She was surprised to see you there, that's all. I'm sorry, Em. That couldn't have been easy."

"What are people saying?"

"What people?"

"Around the office. About my sister being a terrorist."

"You're worried about what people think? No one blames you, but now that we know she won't speak to you, you need to distance yourself from the investigation. Otherwise, Lawson will have your head."

"I can't do that."

"Em, come on. You don't have a choice. Besides, it's for the best, and you know it. I was in there, remember? I heard what you two said to each other. You're too close to this. You can't separate your emotions."

"Being close is not always a bad thing."

"It is in this case. They have rules about personal involvement for a reason."

"I can't give up on her. And Lawson can't keep me away. He has to do what Jep asks. So I can always come at it from that angle."

"Are you listening to yourself?"

"You know what I mean."

"I'm afraid I do. You're going to attempt to use Jep to get what you want. But it won't work."

"What else can I do?"

"Go home if you have to. No one will stop you. Take some time off. Travel. Do whatever it takes to distance yourself from this before you get into trouble. You're not thinking straight."

"If it was *your* sister in there, what would you do?"

"Not this."

"You say that, but we never know how we'll respond to situations we aren't prepared for."

"That's what my training is for," Pearce said. "That's why we didn't want you in the field. There is no agent here who would be as emotionally unstable right now as you are."

"I'm emotionally unstable now? Where's Jep? At least I know he's got my back."

"Does he?"

"Don't even start."

"I'm not starting, Em. I'm concerned."

"Jep's a fantastic agent."

"It's not about that."

"I already told you it was my call to stay in the park."

Pearce looked at the floor. "Sometimes when a civilian has a life-altering experience, they can become…" He sighed.

"What?"

"I've seen it happen before."

"I don't know what you're talking about."

"The way you feel about Jep, it's not real. It's been brought on by your circumstances."

"The way I *feel* about him? What are you saying?"

Jep

"Becoming romantically attached is a normal reaction."

She gasped. "Romantically attached?"

"You have all this trauma you're dealing with, and he's there for you. It even appears to you as if he's saved your life a couple of times."

"You're suggesting— There is nothing going on between Jep and I."

"I know. But do you want it to?"

"No!" She spun around, walking quickly down the hall. "I can't believe you think I'm in love with Jep."

"I have to check. He's a good agent, but he's not against using people to reach his goal. If you're falling for him, it would be easy for him to manipulate that."

"You think he's using me now?"

"I think he's doing what he needs to in order to get the job done."

"I'm glad to know you have so much faith in the two of us."

"Em. I'm sorry."

"I've got work to do, if you'll excuse me."

She reached the elevator and pressed the button several times. "Come on," she said under her breath. It was impossible to know how to respond to Pearce's accusations. She'd had no idea he thought so low of her.

"Em, we have to work together. I wasn't trying to make you uncomfortable, but sometimes we have to face hard truths. If you say there's nothing there, I believe you."

The elevator door opened. "I hear what you're

saying, but give me some time to cool off, and don't ride in the elevator with me."

He lifted his hands in surrender and stepped back. Once the doors closed, she heaved out all her breath. It was a horrifying accusation, but harder given the fact that she was finding it more and more difficult to ignore how she really felt about Jep. And if Pearce was right about her feelings, that was a problem she'd have to face eventually.

Chapter 18

EMERY STARED at the email that had come through from a friend in another department. She hadn't breathed when she'd opened it, but now her breath was releasing in a slow, steady stream. Finally, something had gone right.

The only way she had gotten her mind off her sister —and then what Pearce had said—was to throw herself into her work. Not the work assigned to her by Gardener, but her own. The wait for this email had been agonizing. She'd started her search the day before, as soon as she'd returned to her desk. But now it was here.

Her heart knocked against her chest as she reread the message. It was what she'd been hoping for but thought was impossible to find. It had taken calling in all the favors she had to put the pieces of the puzzle together, but it had paid off.

In the midst of all the horrible things that Jade had said, there was one truth that hit home hard. Em had spent so much time making sure everyone else was happy, she'd forgotten who she was. For all the time she'd spent timidly tiptoeing around the office, trying to play by someone else's rules, it had only taken a life-altering event to push her past her timidity and uncertainty and take control for once. With or without permission.

God, I hope I'm doing the right thing here.

The hard part now was figuring out what her next move would be. She hadn't seen Jep since the day before and had no idea if he was avoiding her or not. Maybe he was thinking the same thing as Pearce about an attachment she'd made. Her cheeks heated at the thought.

She chewed on her thumbnail, then caught herself and tucked her hands in her lap before clicking on the attachment to watch the footage that had been compiled.

As the clips continued, she stopped once in a while to look around the office. She'd found what the others had not, but what should she do with it now? If she brought it to Lawson, he'd lock her out. Pearce would do the same.

There was still one other option. She hurried to her supervisor's office and knocked.

"Em, I was hoping you'd stop by," Gardener said. "I heard what happened, but I didn't want to hound you about it. I figured you'd be getting enough of that."

"Yeah."

"Do you want to come in?"

"If you don't mind."

"I know I'm not the easiest person to get along with, but I'm not heartless. Please, have a seat."

"Thank you."

"I'm so sorry to hear about your sister. I can't imagine what you're going through, but I'm impressed you're straight back to work."

"It's been a shock, but keeping busy helps."

"Have they let you see her?"

"Yesterday. But don't mention it. Lawson doesn't know. Pearce did me a favor."

"You're really leaning into this field work. Well done."

Em was relieved to hear her say so. She'd never found Gardener to be much of an ally. At least some good had come out of all the chaos.

"I'm trying to be more proactive," Em said.

"Did your sister give you anything helpful? Has she told you anything that could help?"

"I thought she would, but she won't talk to me. I had hoped…never mind. It doesn't matter. It is what it is, and I have other skills at my disposal."

"That's a positive angle to take. You have something specific in mind?"

Em bit her lip. "I need to ask a really big favor."

"Sure. Whatever I can do to help the case."

"I found out where Jade's been living. It turns out she's been in the US for almost a year now preparing for this."

Gardener leaned forward a fraction. "You know where she lives? Does Lawson know? How'd you figure it out?"

"Doing what I do best. Looking at the data. I called in a few favors around the place too. But I haven't told anyone else."

"I see. Well done. And what is it you need from me?"

"Lawson wants me off the case, but I want to have a look at her apartment before they move in. Once Lawson knows, he won't let me anywhere near what they find, and I might see something they miss because she's my sister."

"I see. You do know taking you off a case is normal protocol when family is involved, though, right?"

"I know. And I'm not saying they're necessarily wrong…except in this case."

"Em—"

"Please. I know how it sounds. But I only need half a day. Can you cover for me? Tell Lawson you've got me an assignment if he asks? That's all I need from you."

"Can I ask why the sudden change? You've been a disciplined, quiet worker the whole time I've known you. What's happened?"

"I don't know. I guess I'm starting to believe in myself."

"There are easier and safer ways to go about stepping into a new you. Running off to check on the residence of a terrorist is not prudent."

"I have to."

"Can you bring someone with you? Pearce?"

"Pearce wouldn't let me near the place."

"Have you asked?"

"Trust me. We had a falling out of sorts. I don't want to get into it right now."

Jep

"Okay, then what about Jep?"

"I don't know where he is."

Gardener ran her thumbnail along her bottom lip. "I don't see any other way. I won't let you go out on your own."

"Fine, then I'll find Jep and bring him with me."

"Promise?"

"Yes."

"If you can't get ahold of him, don't go."

"I won't."

"And don't make me regret this."

Em smiled. "Thank you. When I get back, I'll fill you in on everything."

"You'd better. No detail is too small."

Em stood and turned for the door, but then stopped. "Do you ever wish you had become an agent instead of an analyst?"

"Me? No way. I don't like participating in the action. I just like to hear about. I am strictly a numbers woman."

"Well, thank you for helping."

"No problem. Go get 'em. Figuratively speaking, of course."

"Of course."

Jep tossed a box aside and leaned over the table, scanning the few items that he'd laid out. They belonged to the man Em had killed.

He lifted a lighter for the second time and held it up

to the light to see the level of the fuel. Half empty. And it had a splatter on it that could have been blood.

After replacing the lighter, he sifted through the pile of coins that were found in the man's coat pocket. Eighty-five cents worth. Could be the change for the unopened packet of gum. But why buy gum if you intend to blow yourself up?

The only other thing he had on him was a flyer with information on a meeting in a local mosque. Jade and the two other deceased suspects had the same thing. The FBI was monitoring the mosque, but after everything that had happened already, they weren't prepared to move on it until they had more information. Jep was already convinced the flyers were a plant intended to send them in the wrong direction.

His phone rang. "Em, how's it going?"

"It's going okay. Where are you? I haven't seen you all day."

"Yeah, sorry. I thought we should give each other space for Lawson's sake. Save a confrontation."

"He also won't let me anywhere near the case, so you wouldn't get much done with me around."

"Also true," Jep said. "Have you spoken to Carla? Did they tell her much?"

"They told her enough. She wasn't very surprised. I guess she saw more of the truth in Jade than I did."

"Pearce told me about your visit with your sister."

"Did he? What did he say?"

"Just that it didn't go well. Sounds like she has some deep wounds from the past that made her easy pickings for extremists."

"Is that all he said?"

"Was there more?"

"Not really." She cleared her throat. "So, what are you up to?"

"I wish I were up to more. I'm going through the personal items we collected from the park. There isn't much."

"I hope they don't move on that flyer. I wouldn't trust anything we get too easily from these people."

"How do you know about the flyer? I thought you weren't supposed to have any contact with this case?"

"I have my sources." He could hear the smirk in Em's voice, and it made him smile. "But the fact that Jade was the only one with a bomb while the others all had weapons says something. Although I don't know exactly what yet."

"That's what I was thinking. That's why we're watching the mosque. Nothing more."

"Good. So…you're not too busy then?"

"Why do you sound like you're hatching a plan?"

"Because I might be."

"I hate to say this to you, but as much as I want to help, and as much as I know you are desperate to be involved, I really do think it's a good idea if you give this investigation a wide berth."

"Not you too."

"It's for your own good."

"I agree with you on a theoretical level, but there are exceptions."

"Like what?"

"Can you meet me at the car?"

Jep paused to consider what she was up to. She was clever, but he'd never thought of her as secretive or conniving. "Why?"

"Because I want to go for a drive."

"Where?"

"It doesn't matter."

"It absolutely does."

"Remember why you chose me as a partner?" Em said.

"Yes."

"Put that at the forefront of your mind, and trust me."

"I do, but I am also apprehensive." He grabbed the box and quickly refilled it. "I'd be more comfortable if you told me where we are going. Or are you afraid I'll turn you in?" He grinned. "I should."

"No you shouldn't. You owe me."

"For what?"

"For almost getting me killed. Twice."

"You said that wasn't my fault."

"It wasn't, but that doesn't mean I won't use it for leverage."

"And you think I'll be willing to put you in danger again?"

"I won't be in danger."

"That's what you said at the park."

"This is different," Em said. "There is no danger. I promise. Are you going to meet me at the car or not?"

Jep paused before leaving the room. "Tell me what you have, or I'm not going."

"Fine, then I'll go on my own."

Jep

He groaned. "You're the worst."

"Does that mean you're coming?"

"I can be there in ten."

He gave his phone a dirty look once he'd hung up, but really, he was proud of her. When they'd first met, she'd been timid about trusting herself. That had all changed. Hopefully for the better, but he'd reserve his judgment on that until after this next outing.

Em was leaning against the car when Jep arrived.

"Where are we going?" he said, holding his thumb on the key fob but not pressing it yet.

Em pulled on the handle, then lifted her eyebrows. "You going to unlock it?"

"Tell me where we're going."

"When we're on the road."

"Why can't you tell me now?"

"Because I want to make sure you don't leave without me."

"I knew it." He unlocked the car.

"Knew what?"

"That this was a bad idea. I've created a monster."

"*You've* created a monster?"

"Yeah. I take full responsibility. I opened that can of worms."

"Yup. And there's no way to put them back." She tucked her shoulder up to her chin in a cheeky gesture, then got in the car. He rolled his eyes and followed suit.

"At least you're smiling," he said when he started the car.

"It helps when you feel like you're getting somewhere."

"So you really do have a lead?"

"I do. And it's big."

"For the last ten minutes," Jep said, pulling out of the parking spot, "I've been wracking my brain, trying to figure out what you could possibly have that no one else has figured out yet."

"You don't think I could come up with something the others couldn't?"

"I have no doubt you could. But what would warrant you sneaking out with me? You said it wasn't dangerous, but you're not going on your own."

"Maybe it's not for protection. Maybe I like your company."

He shook his head and pulled onto the street. "You're telling me there's absolutely no chance of danger?"

She pressed her lips together and nodded.

"And yet," he said. "You were afraid if you told me where we were going, I'd leave you behind."

"Okay, so maybe there is a slight chance of danger, but it's very slight. Almost imperceptible."

"I don't believe you. So, we're on the road now. Where are going?"

"Turn right up here."

"That's it? You're going to give me directions?"

"We're going to an apartment building."

"Where someone lives?"

"Not right at this very moment, but yes."

He looked at her when he stopped at the red light. "Don't tell me you've discovered where Jade's been living."

"As a matter of fact…"

"How?"

"By doing the job I was hired to do. I gathered the data and put it together."

"Does anyone else know?"

"A couple of low-level guys who helped me with traffic cams. Although they don't know whose address it was they helped me find. And Gardener knows because I needed her to cover for me."

"Gardener agreed to cover for you? I don't know how you do it."

"Do what?"

"Get people to do things for you."

"The traffic guys owed me a favor, and Gardener isn't so bad once you get to know her. I think this case has made everyone step outside of their usual lines. We all want these guys. We're all willing to do what's necessary, even if it's unconventional. Even Lawson."

"He's going to be furious when he finds out where you've gone."

"Maybe, but he'll be happy about what we find, and I'm sure that will soften him up."

"There's no softening up Lawson."

"Everything softens with a bit of warmth."

"Not rocks. They crack when they're heated."

"Okay, so it wasn't the best analogy."

"You're also assuming we find what we need. We

might not. They could have cleared out. Or they could have left us evidence we're supposed to find like before."

"They were carrying what they wanted us to find. And Jade's had ample opportunity to tell us if that's what they wanted us to know."

"If you shared your discovery with Lawson, he'd already have a team over there collecting every fiber."

"I know. That's why I'm getting in there first. What if I see something they won't?"

"Okay. I hear what you're saying, but I'll tell you what, there was one thing you were definitely right about."

"What's that?"

"If you had told me where we were going before we got in the car, I would have left you behind."

"See? I've got you all figured out, Jep Booth."

"You think so?"

"I do. You're that easy to read."

"Oh yeah? Tell me what I'm thinking right now."

Em smirked. "That if this job doesn't kill me, you might."

"Wow, you didn't hesitate with that answer at all."

"Am I right?"

"You are good."

"Told ya."

Except killing her was the last thing on his mind at that moment. He sent a quick glance her way. Long enough to notice the soft curve of her upturned lips. Then he focused on the road.

Chapter 19

JEP CONTINUED DOWN THE STREET, slowing as they passed the apartment building.

"Keep your eyes peeled. Let me know anything you see that's unusual," he said.

"I know the drill. Looks clear to me."

Jep did a loop, then parked at the end of the block and watched the building in the rearview mirror.

"How long do we have to wait here?" she said.

"As long as it takes."

"No one's there."

"What makes you so sure?"

She craned her neck around until she spotted the camera. "There." She pointed. "Footage from that camera has shown no lights on in the apartment since the park incident. Everyone who was living there is either dead or in custody. I got footage of the previous weeks and identified all four suspects coming and going. Never with anyone else."

"When did you have time to do all this?"

"I didn't. The computers did. Once I had entered the identities of the suspects, all that was left for me to do was to view the footage that had them in it."

"But you can't be sure. What would you have done if you came here alone?"

"Knocked on the door. If someone answered, I'd tell them I was looking for Bob and they'd tell me I have the wrong apartment. Easy. Then Lawson could have brought a team in."

"That's not a bad plan." He frowned because he didn't like it making sense for her to go into the field on her own.

When he reached for the door handle, so did she.

"Hang on a second," he said, grabbing her arm.

"I'm not staying in the car, if that's what you're thinking."

"I'd rather you did."

"I'm sure you would, but you're only here because of the information I provided. And we agreed my eyes on this would be helpful."

"That is all true, but now that we're here—"

"Jade's my sister, so I'm going in."

"What does her being your sister have to do with anything?"

Em took a deep breath. "The stuff she said when I saw her was…difficult. It wasn't the picture I had painted of her for so long. I need to see. I need to understand what drove her to the place she's at now. How she could fall into this deep, depressing hole where she became willing to carry out atrocities."

Jep

"Have you considered that you might not like what you find?"

"I still want to know. I need to. So unless you handcuff me to the steering wheel, I'm going in."

"I do have handcuffs."

"You wouldn't dare."

"Maybe not, but that doesn't stop me from considering it. I'll tell you what. If you let me go in first and clear the apartment, I'll come back and get you."

"Okay, deal." She reached for the door handle again.

"You said you'd wait."

"What? Here? Why?"

"Because that's what we agreed on."

"I'll wait in the lobby." She got out before he could grab her again.

"You are impossible," he mumbled as he got out of the car and followed her to the front door. "Let me check the lobby first."

"You think someone's waiting for us on the other side of that door?"

He gave her a look that she must have understood, because she leaned against the brick wall and sulked.

"Thank you," he said as someone came out, and he slipped inside before the door closed.

It was a small space with a vinyl parquet floor curling on itself at the corners.

A cluster of mailboxes was set into one wall next to a flight of stairs leading up. He opened a door in the other wall and found another flight of stairs that led into a dark basement. He would have checked it if he hadn't remembered Em's words about the probability someone was waiting for them. If it had been just him on site, he wouldn't have bothered because he was sure it was clear. When Lawson sent a team in, they'd tear the place apart if they had to.

He opened the front door and tucked his head out. "You can come in now."

"Didn't find any scary monsters?"

"Funny."

"I thought so." She joined him inside. "You know how to pick locks, right?"

"Why do I suddenly feel like that's the only reason you brought me?"

"That's not the reason. I know how to pick locks."

"You do not."

"I do," Em said.

"Where'd you learn?"

"Tell you what, you clear the apartment so I can come have a look, and I'll tell you then."

He glanced at the mailboxes. "Deal. But I want to see you in action. Open the mailbox. What's the apartment number?"

"Two-oh-four."

He handed her a lock pick set, and she got to work.

"Give me some room," she said, nudging her shoulder back into his chest.

He shifted a little but remained perched over her shoulder.

"Not bad," he said when the door popped open.

"Not bad, but it's empty. Hopefully we'll have better luck upstairs."

"It shouldn't take me long, but pull out your phone."

"Why?"

"If anyone comes in, you need to have a reason for standing here. Being distracted on your phone is as good a reason as any."

She dragged it from her pocket and waggled it in front of him. "Ready and waiting."

"I'll come get you once I know it's safe." He took one more look at her before he headed up the stairs.

His boots scuffed on the threadbare carpet as he canvased the hall. The one light that illuminated the dim hall flickered, drawing attention to the peeling wallpaper and stains he'd rather not try to identify.

When he reached the apartment, he knocked and turned his back in case someone looked through the peephole. When there was no response, he waited and listened before picking the lock.

With his gun in hand, he turned the knob, stepping out of a direct line of sight as he pushed the door opened. The silence continued besides the *doof-doof* coming from another apartment.

After another beat, he entered, taking minimal notice of the contents of the rooms as he cleared them.

A square wooden table in the kitchen was full of what looked like bomb-making material, but he'd confirm that later. A wall in the living area was covered in newspaper articles. On the floor, against another wall, was an unmade mattress. It looked like someone had been sleeping on the couch as well.

He moved into the one bedroom and found it empty besides a double bed and a plain bedside table that had several books about ending Western tyranny as well as a large statue of a figure holding a knife in the air, waiting to strike. The bed was made.

The closet and the bathroom had a few personal items and toothbrushes that would make it easy to get DNA.

He went back to the living room but hesitated before leaving. He wanted to call the team in right away, but he couldn't do that to Em. He was also curious to know her thoughts on the apartment. There wasn't much, but he wouldn't be surprised if she noticed something no one else would.

Em was scrolling through the latest news when Jep came back downstairs.

"We're clear," he said. "You ready?" He tossed her a pair of latex gloves.

"How's it look?" She stretched the rubber over her fingers while Jep did the same.

"Like you'd expect. Not much in the way of personal items, but you might know better."

Em nodded and followed him up the stairs, but she stopped when they reached the doorway.

"You okay?" Jep said.

"I don't know what I was expecting. Growing up, she had posters of her favorite bands all over the walls. Now there are newspaper articles."

She walked over and tilted her head as she read

several of the headlines. "I don't recognize any of these stories."

"That's because they're likely all cover-ups. Like this." He pointed at an article on the edge of the clutter. "Explosion from gas leak."

"I know that one." She looked through the dates. "Most of these were from before my time on the task force. Were you a part of the team during any of these events?"

"Some of them. But we were successful. As we get more current, the agency fell farther and farther behind."

"Then they knew. All of them." She gestured across the wall. "They knew what all of these were. Whoever is behind this recent stuff has a connection to the past."

"They've been studying us for a long time."

Jep leaned over to lift a notebook he spotted poking out from underneath the mattress on the floor. "Do you know if this is your sister's handwriting?" He handed it to her.

She flipped through a few pages. "I don't think so. Her letters are more loopy. But we've got the postcards, so a handwriting expert can look at it." She read a couple of lines. "It's really hard to read." She flipped through to the last page and deciphered what she could. "There's a lot of not very nice things said about all of us."

Jep walked beside her so he could read it. "I'm sure none of that is about you."

"Every law enforcement type in here, including me."

"From what I can make out, whoever this belongs to,

they've been chronicling their plan. This could be exactly what we need to bust this thing wide open."

"I sure hope so." She handed him the notebook and went to the table. "But I think we have a greater concern right now."

"What's that?"

She pointed at the kitchen table. "This is all for making bombs. But not the vest Jade was wearing."

Jep scanned the paraphernalia that littered the table and the empty bottles on the floor. "You know about bombs?"

"I know enough. I read a lot of reports. Whatever they were making, it looks like a lot, and none of it is here anymore."

"We need to call the team in," Jep said. "We can't afford to wait any longer."

"Not even five minutes? I'm almost done." Em moved to the fridge and opened it. "I'll make sure I'm out of the way before—hang on."

"What is it?"

She pulled out a container. "Hot dogs."

"So, not Muslims then."

"It doesn't make sense. Someone must have been, look at the literature around the place. But if you haven't given yourself fully over to it, why risk your life?"

"If there are multiple players, that could make things complicated. Different motives. There are plenty of people who would get involved if the price is right. Or if they have something against law enforcement. Hey, you haven't told me about your lock picking prowess," Jep said as he picked up a pamphlet off the couch.

Jep

"Oh that. It's not very interesting. It was one of the courses I took."

"Were you planning on doing fieldwork?"

"No, I thought it would be fun. Also, if I ever locked myself out of the house, I wouldn't have to call the locksmith. I was good too."

"I bet you were." He read through the pamphlet and tossed it aside. "Why do the nations rage and the people plot in vain?" he mumbled.

"What?"

"Nothing."

"You quoted the Bible."

"I know."

"Psalm two."

"Verse one," he said. "I know."

"*You* know scripture?"

"Should I not?"

"I didn't expect you to be so studied up, but I guess it's important as an agent to know about all religions."

He laughed lightly and scratched his eyebrow. "I don't know scripture for my job. I'm not that disciplined about work."

"Then what's it for?"

"It's bread for life. I couldn't do without it."

Em blinked a few times as she tried to make sense of what he'd said. All of her assumptions about him lined up and were staring her in the face. She'd been very, very wrong. "You're a Christian."

"That's a shock to you." The small curve at the edge of his mouth embarrassed her. He was amused by her ignorance instead of offended. He wasn't bothered in the slightest by the misunderstanding, but part of her wished he had been. That it mattered to him.

"I hate to admit that it is," she said, tossing the hotdogs back into the fridge and closing it.

"You didn't expect a guy like me could have a personal relationship with Jesus?"

"It—" ...challenged everything she thought she knew about him, and now she had to revisit every conversation they'd had and every action he'd taken.

"Don't worry about it," he said. "It's not like I ever offered you that information. And we all have our prejudices. Even the disciples. None of us is perfect."

"I'm an idiot. I made up my mind about you too soon. I'm sorry."

"I said don't worry about it."

"I do. I should know better. I'm actually a Christian too."

"I figured."

"You did not. You're just saying that to make me feel bad."

He laughed. "I'm really not. It's the way you talk and your God-given gift of discernment."

"Now you're picking on me."

"Maybe a little." His smile dropped from his face at the same time his head jerked to the side.

"What—" was all Em could get out before he dove for her, knocking her to the floor and crushing the air from her lungs. Shots exploded into the room, and she tried to scream, but she had no breath left.

Chapter 20

JEP ROLLED off of Em and pulled his gun as the door was kicked in. He fired, pushing their assailants back.

"Get to the bedroom." He shoved her forward. "I'll be right behind you." He fired a few more rounds as he scrambled after her, putting himself between her and their attackers.

He slammed the bedroom door shut and dove beside the bed as a volley of bullets tore into the walls. Scrambling up to his knees, he shot at the door, then bumped the bedside table, knocking the statue to the floor, where it shattered.

"Stay down," he said as he dragged the bed away from the wall. A shard of statue cut into his knee when he had to duck again to avoid being shot.

Em crawled around to help him push the bed into place before more shots were fired, ripping the door apart.

Jep fired again as he pulled Em toward the window. "Go."

"You can't stay here."

"I'll be right behind you. Just go."

She hesitated only a second before making her move.

"Don't die," she said as she climbed onto the fire escape and ducked out of sight.

Jep duck-walked to the window, keeping his head out of the firing line.

"Get out of there!" she yelled.

"Go down to the street and wait for me there out of sight."

The shots kept coming. Jep returned fire before diving out the window. He slammed against the rail, and it gave way, sending him rolling off the platform.

"Jep!" Em screamed from the ladder.

He hung in the air, his hand gripping a broken bit of railing as his gun clattered to the ground.

They were almost eye level, and they looked at each other before Jep checked the window, then looked back at her. "Get out of here. You have to go. Now."

"I can't. The ladder's broken."

He checked to see that the bottom half was missing. It was a long way to the ground.

He kept his voice calm. "You have to jump."

She squeezed her eyes shut as she shook her head in furious rotation. "It's too far."

"Em. Look at me." She did. "You have to do this. They will kill you. Please. Go. Now."

She licked her lips and slowly unwrapped her arm from around the rung before descending until she dangled off the bottom of the ladder.

Jep

"Jump!" he yelled.

She made a squeaking noise as she let go and hit the ground with a thud, her legs collapsing under her.

Jep swung sideways and hooked his leg on the ladder where she had been. "Run!" He yelled at her as he pulled himself across. Although, the way she'd fallen, he wasn't sure that she could.

A figure appeared at the window, and Jep opened his mouth to yell again when a shot was fired from below, and the man disappeared again. He hugged the ladder and looked to see Em sitting on the ground, pointing his gun at the window.

"Come on," she called up to him. "You're clear. Hurry."

He slid the rest of the way down the ladder and landed near Em with a roll.

She fired again before he took the gun from her.

"They could cut us off at the road," he said. "We need to go. Can you walk?"

She pushed up but grimaced. "I don't know."

He kept an eye on the window and kept checking the end of the alley as he wrapped his free arm around her and dragged her to her feet. "I wish I could leave you where you are until an ambulance turns up, but we don't have a choice, I'm afraid. I'm gonna need you to try. Otherwise, you can jump on my back."

He fired at the window again as she put more weight on her legs and limped forward. "I can do it."

"You sure?"

"Yeah." She limped faster to prove the point.

He kept his arm around her, hating that he had to drag her faster, but she didn't cry out in pain.

Once they were around the corner, he confirmed there were no hostiles in his line of sight and leaned her against the wall while he made a call.

"Agents in distress. We need backup now. Multiple assailants." After giving them the address, he tucked his phone back into his pocket and pulled off the latex gloves that were torn to pieces. Em looked at her hands, suddenly remembering them.

"We need to find somewhere safe to hide you."

"Can we go back to the car and get out of here?" She pulled off what was left of the rubber.

"They could be watching. And I'm not ready to leave yet. Can you keep walking?"

She took a few steps, scrunching her face in pain, but nodded.

"Stay low," he said, pushing her in front of him while he watched behind them. After rounding a corner, he checked doors until he found one that was unlocked. "In here," he said, checking the street before shutting them both inside.

"What if they find us in here?" she said, looking around the small foyer of what appeared to be a boutique suite of offices, but there was no one around.

An emerald daybed with gold buttons was in a small nook, and the tiled floor displayed some kind of star pattern whose rays reached out to the walls.

"They won't. They weren't following."

"How'd they even know we were here?"

"Someone was either watching, or they were tipped off."

"By who?"

"Your guess is as good as mine. For now, I won't take any chances. We'll need to find a hiding place for you until backup arrives."

"Why just for me? You're not going back out there, are you?"

His face crumpled in frustration. "We need the journal."

She tipped her head toward the ceiling. "I forgot about the journal."

"I must have dropped it when I dove for you back at the kitchen."

"Then we can go back for it when the others arrive. It's too dangerous to go get it now."

"We can't wait. It may already be too late, but I have to try." His eyes pivoted across the room to a door with a gold nameplate that read "Janitor".

"Over here," he said, taking her hand.

"You want me to hide in a janitor's closet?"

He opened the door, and the faint smell of bleach greeted them.

"There isn't room," Em said, nudging a bucket with her toe.

"You can climb on top of those boxes."

She pursed her lips. "I'm not sitting on a pile of cardboard. I can come with you."

"No way." He scooped her up, and she yelped as he deposited her on a box that half-collapsed under her weight. "I can't do my job if I'm worried about you. Especially when you're struggling to walk."

"So I'm supposed to sit here and worry?"

"No. You can sit and pray. If I don't come find you in an hour, you can come out."

"But—"

He shut her into the dark, pressing his hand on the outside of the door when she yelled.

"Jep! Jep, I don't like this! You'd better come back to me when this is all over." Her voice trailed off at the end. He mouthed the word "sorry," then turned and ran to the door, checking how many rounds he had left.

"Three," he said as he replaced the magazine. He couldn't risk going to the car for more, so three would have to be enough.

"God, I'm going to need you to go before me on this one," he said as he hurried down the sidewalk, taking notice of every pedestrian and vehicle that approached.

The journal would be helpful, but taking one of these guys alive could also be invaluable.

He ducked into a doorway to stay out of sight as he scanned the street and the front of the building. It was the only way in. For now, it was clear.

As he moved to approach the building, he kept his gun pressed against his leg to keep it from being seen too easily by anyone who shouldn't. He waited until a car drove past before running for the building, noting, as he pushed open the front door, that it was broken. Whoever had attacked them hadn't had a key. He deposited that piece of information to contemplate later as he slipped inside.

A horn blared somewhere on the street, and he twisted sideways, pressing against the wall. He waited a breath before checking through the window that filled the top half of the door, then made his way to the stairs.

Focusing on the molded texture of the gun grip as it pressed into his palm, he climbed. His increased heart rate throbbed through his chest, beating out a quick, steady rhythm that faded from thought when he reached the top of the stairs and did a quick check of the hall.

He stepped slowly onto the empty landing. The front door of the apartment had been shredded by bullets and was hanging from one hinge. He ducked to get a view of the kitchen beyond. If the journal was still there, it would be on the floor somewhere in the kitchen. He shifted to get a different view of the room. It appeared to be empty. Hopefully, they were all out combing the streets. He thought of Em in the closet. He had been content leaving her there. She should be safe, but nothing was ever certain in these situations. Especially where Em was concerned. She was a magnet for disaster, but she'd somehow come out on top. If God was in this… "God, let the journal be there."

He took one step but was thrown back against the wall when a flash was followed by an explosion.

A heavy darkness hung in the air with the tangy smoke that stuck in his lungs, refusing to budge as he tried to take a breath. Bells rung in muted procession through his head, and his vision cleared to a vague blur as his throat tugged uselessly for breath.

He rolled onto his side and dragged himself toward

the stairs while his diaphragm finally responded in small gulps of air to a drowning man.

He pulled himself down a step, then slid down a couple more in thumps, which must have dislodged something because his diaphragm released in a rush. He sputtered and heaved, continuing to slide down the steps until he reached the bottom, where he laid on the landing, stretching his face to clear his eyes from their prison of fog. He ignored the high and low tones of ringing, considering that he was alive when his body was telling him he should be dead.

He rolled onto his arms with a groan, noticing for the first time that his gun was still in his hand. Using the little bit of strength that was returning to him, he put the weapon back into his holster before pushing up onto his knees, then attempted to rise to his feet.

After the initial dizzy spell, his head cleared further, and he staggered to the front door, stumbling outside, where people were gathering, gaping.

"Hey," someone said, walking up to him but not touching him. "You okay? What happened in there?"

All Jep could think was that people asked the weirdest questions.

He shook away the fuzz and pushed past the man as he surveyed the scene. More people were moving toward the explosion, their phones lifted to the smoke pouring out a window on the second floor. But one man was moving abruptly away from the scene and around the corner.

More people were talking to him, but he couldn't afford to change his attention in any other direction. It

Jep

took all he had to remain focused on the corner. His legs moved almost of their own accord to follow his line of sight. His gait gaining speed as his body recognized itself again.

He pulled his weapon when he reached the corner and the sound of sirens pierced through the pinging bells in his ears. Behind him, the crowd had forgotten about him and were focused on the fire that was now breaking windows.

He rounded the corner with his weapon raised, checking doorways and alleys as he moved forward. Then, as he passed another alley, he saw the toe of a shoe disappear behind a dumpster.

He aimed and approached. Slowly. Quietly. His training driving him forward in stealth and precision despite his condition. The man was his. Jep was ready. Coiled. But his ears still hummed, so he didn't hear the woosh from behind, and there was no time to react before another flash sent him into a void.

Chapter 21

"JEP?" He felt a sharp jolt at his cheek. "Agent Booth?"

He fought against the darkness, but it was slow to recede. The apartment exploding came back, and he wondered if he'd dreamed the rest.

"Jep? You okay? Wake up." Another slap. He blinked his eyes open and saw the sky above and a shadowy figure perched above him. "There you are. Welcome back to the land of the living. I thought maybe your pulse was lying. You look like a corpse."

"Pearce?"

"Hey, buddy. You just lie there. The paramedics are on their way."

Jep's eyes shifted to look around and make sense of his surroundings, but it sent a shock of pain through his skull, and he closed his eyes. "What happened?"

"It's hard to say. You're a mess. Among other things, I'd say you got a nasty bump on the head."

Jep pushed up onto his elbows, and the pounding in his head sent bile into his throat.

Jep

"Hey," Pearce said. "Slow down. There's nowhere you need to be. I'd hate to think what's on the ground in this alley, but that's the least of your worries. Try not to think about it and lie still."

"No." Jep touched the side of his head. There was no blood, but there was a sizable lump. "I'll be okay."

He sat up farther, pausing to let the giddiness pass before getting the rest of the way up. "I'm gonna feel this in the morning."

"Aren't you feeling it now?" Pearce said, holding his arm at his elbow to steady him.

"You know how it is when you're on the job. No time to feel anything." Jep looked up the alley. "His friend must have been watching and followed me."

"Who?"

"You would have noticed the explosion?"

"It's hard to miss. Was that you?"

"Not directly, but I almost got caught up in it. I was outside the door."

"Whoa. No wonder you look like you do. You must be a cat. How many lives do you have left?"

"I think my ledger might be in the red."

"Were you on your own? Should we be looking out for anyone else? When you made the call, it sounded like you said agents, not agent."

Jep almost gave Emery away but caught himself. "Just me. I was checking on a lead. How long was I out?"

"Not long, but I don't know how long you were knocked out before that. We arrived just after the firetrucks. What was the lead you were checking out?"

"Emery called me and told me she had found her sister's address. She wanted me to check it out."

"That's Jade's place that's up in smoke? So you didn't get a chance to look inside?"

"We—I did. But they must have been watching because I was ambushed. Had to escape out the window and left a journal behind that looked like it would be helpful. I doubled back to get it and got a face full of bomb instead. I'm hoping there's something left to be salvaged."

"Won't have any luck there. It's blown to smithereens. What the bomb didn't destroy the fire did. Nothing left. You're lucky you're alive."

"Yeah." Jep squeezed the back of his neck. "That journal would have been our best lead yet. It looked like it had details in it that could have been invaluable."

"You had a look at it? Can you remember of the details?"

"No. It was hard to make out the writing. We would have needed someone to look at it. The few things I could make out weren't enough to get us anywhere."

Pearce sighed. "We can't seem to get a break in this investigation."

"They had bomb-making materials in there as well, so there's a chance another attack is coming."

"You let me worry about. You've had a big day already. Let's get you looked at. We'll still be here when you get back."

"I don't need to see anyone. There's too much to do. I've got some stuff I need to look into."

Jep

"What? Jep, come on, you're injured. What's more important than looking after yourself?"

"I'll stop in to see the doctor later."

"Where are you going?"

"It's a personal matter."

"Right now?" It was clear Pearce wasn't convinced.

"Yeah."

"If I give you some advice, will you take it?"

"I'll listen," Jep said. "That's all I can offer."

"Lawson's going to be livid when he finds out about how this all unfolded. You and I both know you should have run it by him before coming here. If we had brought a team first—"

"Lawson will live."

"You've made quite a mess with very little to show for it. The best thing you can do right now is to lie low."

"I'm not planning on making another move today."

"You should be taking this more seriously. This doesn't look good."

"You should know by now I don't care about looks."

Pearce shook his head. "Fine. It's your head."

"I'll see you later."

Em didn't know if it was the chemical smells that were making her dizzy or fear. When the building had shaken, she'd known it was a bomb. She tried to quiet the shouts in her head, insisting that Jep was dead. But in the dark, all she had for company were her thoughts, unwilling to obey her command. She squeezed her eyes shut, trying to fend off the pounding in her head. She needed air. But leaving the closet also meant she'd have to face what was out there.

"God, give me the strength." Her voice sounded hollow in the close space. She shifted on the box, sending a shock of pain down her legs, not from the jump off the fire escape but from the pins and needles that had started twenty minutes before. She couldn't stay here forever.

Her hand felt down the door in the dark and wrapped around the knob. "You can do this." She needed light and air or she'd go crazy.

Before she could turn the knob, the door gave way under her hand, and so did the box underneath her. She tumbled sideways, but the figure that met her in the light caught her.

"Whoa. Hey," Jep said. "Looks like I turned up right on time."

She hung awkwardly from his arms as he tried to help her stand, but her legs wouldn't cooperate, and she was so overwhelmed by the sight of him that she dislodged her arms from his grip and wrapped them around his neck, holding tight while she cried into his shoulder.

"You're not dead," she said into the warmth of his shirt.

"No. I'm okay. It's okay." He ran a hand over her head and rested it on her back. "You're shaking. Everything's okay."

"I thought you were dead. Was there a bomb? I thought I felt a bomb."

Jep

"Yeah, but I'm okay."

She held on until it edged on too long, then tested her toes on the floor. "I don't know if I can stand."

He carried her to the emerald couch and sat her down before bending down to prod her ankles, palpating up her calf. "Where does it hurt? I don't see any swelling or bruising." He looked up at her.

"Jep!" It was the first chance she had to get a good look at him. "What happened to you?" His hair was a mess and grayed from what looked like powder. "You've got blood on your face."

"I'm fine. I wouldn't be here if I wasn't. We need to get your legs looked at."

"The pain isn't from the fall, it's from sitting in that closet too long. I'm all pins and needles. It'll pass."

"Are you sure? The way you fell, I expected a fracture, especially after you had to walk. We need to get x-rays. Just in case."

"But there's no swelling."

"Yeah." He made another pass over her other leg.

"Forget about my legs. Are we safe? Tell me what happened to you."

"The explosion was in the apartment. It went off as I approached the door."

She closed her eyes and rested her head on the back of the couch. "I couldn't stop thinking you were dead."

"I guess God's not done with me yet. Unfortunately, I couldn't get the journal."

"I'm just glad you're alive."

"You're not at all disappointed that we've got nothing?"

"Are you kidding? The journal never even crossed my mind. I mean, I know it was important, but not at the expense of your life. Allow me a moment to celebrate the fact that you are here right now, living and breathing."

He bit his lip while the corners of his mouth turned up, and he looked at her from under his brow. She couldn't remember a time when a man had looked at her like that.

"By all means," he said. "Take your time."

"Good. Thank you." A silence opened up that embarrassed her, but he teased her with a charmingly crooked grin.

"All right. That's enough," she said, pushing up off the couch. "I think I'm good now."

"You sure? I can wait."

"Yes, that was plenty."

"It's not often a beautiful woman celebrates my life. I have a birthday once a year you could commemorate if you like."

"Me and my big mouth."

"You ready to get out of here?"

"Yes, please." She held his arm as they walked to the door until she was confident she could do it on her own. "So that's it then? You almost died, and we got nothing?"

"I came close to catching one of them."

"When?"

"After the explosion. I saw him fleeing the scene and followed him. I had him cornered, but his friend came in from behind and knocked me out."

"Why didn't you tell me?" She pulled him to a stop and looked at him again. Reassessing. "You're lucky he didn't kill you."

"I think our backup arrived before he could."

"Another miracle."

"We've had a few of those lately."

"But not the kind that gives us the answers we need," she said.

"We don't know that for sure."

"I don't think my sister will ever talk, and if there are bombs out there somewhere, who knows what's coming? And there's nothing we can do to stop it."

"We both got a good look at what was in the apartment. I think we should go over it again."

"But you said it's all gone."

"Yeah, but there could be other clues." He tapped her head. "Up here. Something to tell us where to look next."

"I can't remember anything important."

"You've also been stuck in a closet, frozen in fear. We need to clear our heads and take the time to think back to before we were interrupted in the apartment."

"Interrupted? That's a mild word for it."

"There might be something we missed. Something we didn't have the time to process."

"It's worth a shot."

"Great," he said. "Let's get back to the office—actually, that might not be a good idea. I'm not ready to face Lawson yet, and he definitely won't give us any time to think."

"Good point. And the place will be crazy. Someplace

quiet would be better. My head is spinning. I think I'm high off the fumes from that closet."

"What about your place?"

"I have a better idea." She checked her watch. "My aunt has a lovely little garden in her backyard. It's one of my favorite places, and she won't be home right now. It would be a really good spot to clear our heads."

"Does she have coffee?"

"Yes."

"Perfect. Let's go."

Chapter 22

"I MOVED IN HERE when I was ten," Em said as she unlocked the front door. She stepped across the threshold and inhaled the familiar scent of eucalyptus and raspberry.

"Were you and your aunt close before that?"

"No. We almost never saw her. I found out later that my mom tried to keep her away from us."

"Why would she do that?"

"I think she was afraid we'd like Carla better."

"And she lost you to your aunt in the end anyway."

"She didn't have to." Em lead him past a cozy living room and into a small kitchen. "Carla tried to bring us back together. When she took us in, it was only meant to be temporary. Just to give my mom time to get her life sorted out."

"She never did?"

"She fell deeper into depression, ended up addicted to painkillers. I visited her once when I was sixteen. She was living in a tiny studio apartment. I barely recognized her. After neither one of us said much over thirty minutes, I left knowing it was the last time I'd see her. She died a year later of a stroke. A small mercy, I think."

"I'm sorry."

"God knew what he was doing bringing me to Carla. She's the reason I found my faith. She started bringing me to church, and I never looked back— I'm sorry, but have you seen yourself in the mirror?"

He raked his hand through his hair, yanking at the end to get his fingers through. "I'm avoiding it as long as I can."

"Why don't you go into the bathroom and clean up. I can't concentrate with you looking like that."

"It's that bad?"

"You look like a corpse."

"That's what Pearce said when he found me. All right. I'll go make myself presentable. Through there?" He pointed down the hall.

"Yeah. Second door on the left. There are fresh towels in the closet across the hall."

"Thanks."

She took the creamer from the fridge and pulled the coffee machine from a cupboard, plugging in on the counter before retrieving a couple of pods from a drawer.

The pipes groaned for a couple of seconds as the shower started. They always had. She hugged the pods to her chest and smiled. There was something cozy and safe about being here with Jep. It was normal. Easy.

Once the water turned off, she popped the first pod into the machine and started it. She was leaning against

Jep

the counter when he emerged with damp hair and a clean face, and she almost sighed. "Coffee?"

"Yes, please."

She focused on the drink as she handed it to him, afraid the look on her face would give her away.

He took the cup and breathed in the steam. "This is exactly what I needed. So was that shower."

"Here's the creamer and sugar." She set them up on the counter next to where he sat on a stool.

He added a splash of cream. "You'll have to show me where Carla keeps the vacuum. I shook out my clothes without thinking, and now there's a thin film covering the floor."

"Don't worry about it. I'll take care of it." She put in another pod and waited while it hummed and gurgled. "I got this coffee maker for my aunt for Christmas, but she never uses it."

"Why did you get her a coffee machine if she doesn't drink coffee?"

"She drinks instant. Always has. I thought I could convert her, but she insists it tastes better."

Jep snorted. "To each his own."

"So…I'm curious."

"About?"

"*Your* faith."

"You want more stories?"

"Yeah. I'm interested to know where it began. After growing up the way you did, how'd you find God?"

"It was messy."

"Too messy to share? It's okay if you don't want to."

"No. It's not a secret. I was hallucinating and stepped off the roof of a five-story building."

"What? Are you being serious?"

"Yeah."

"Wh—how?"

"A girl dumped me, and I was not handling it well. A friend of mine had access to the roof of this building where we used to hang out and get high. I went up there to stew and…maybe it was the drugs or maybe it was the devil—probably both—but a black fog settled around me and whispered seductive darkness into my ear."

Em leaned on the counter. "What was it saying?"

"I couldn't hear words, exactly. It was more the sense of despair that soaked into my pores. Then it felt like I was lifted off the ground and carried to the edge of the roof. When I looked over, I saw a pool of black, and all I wanted to do was fall in. Swim around in it."

She shook her head. "You must have been in a very dark place to want more darkness."

"I think we all do it now and then. Something gets you down, and you let your thoughts spiral. It's an odd comfort wallowing in self-pity and misery."

"That's true. I've never been that low, but there have been times when I've been down, and there is a pull to go deeper into the mire. It's almost like if you can justify your pain, then circumstances will have to change. But then they don't, and you've got to climb out again. Or you jump off a roof— So what happened? You obviously didn't jump."

"I did."

Jep

She jerked upright. "Wait—so—"

"I leaned forward. Let all my weight drag me into the abyss, but someone yanked me back onto the roof."

"Who was it? Did your friend turn up?"

Jep took a sip. "I have no idea. Next thing I knew, I was on my back looking up at the cloudy sky. No one else was there. I watched the clouds for a minute. They moved slowly, but then…they just parted, and a ray of sun pierced through. I stared at it, somehow knowing that it was for me, and this voice, deep inside, said, 'My son—'" He pressed his lips together against his emotion and took another sip. "He said, 'My son, if you ask the darkness to hide you, if the surrounding light became night, even in the darkness you cannot hide from me. I will always find you.'"

Em sniffed against her own tears. "Psalm 139."

"Yeah. I didn't know that at the time, but I knew who it was speaking to me. When I got up from that roof, I was a changed man. I left my old life behind and started a new one."

"That's incredible."

"And imagine my surprise when I started reading the Bible and came across Psalm 139."

"What did you think? That must have been—amazing."

"I read it over and over and over, not because I was surprised, exactly. I knew by then what God was capable of, but even now—telling that story—it gives me goosebumps."

Em rubbed her arm. "Me too."

"Does that mean you've accepted me into the fold?

No longer confounded by my being a Christian?" he teased.

"I was never confounded."

"You were too. You should have seen the look on your face."

"Okay, maybe a little. And I'm sorry. I did judge you. On more than one occasion, you've surprised me. Whereas you seem to know me very well."

"My background puts me in a better position to not judge others."

"It shouldn't matter. There's no excuse for it."

He shrugged. "None of us is perfect."

"You're a good man, Jep. Whatever anyone says. I'm glad they brought you back to the team." She held her mug in two hands while she gulped too fast against a rising feeling she was unprepared for. She welcomed the scalding heat as it pulled her feet back to the earth.

"That caffeine kicking in yet?" Jep said.

"Almost. Give me another couple of minutes and I'll be ready."

"A few minutes it is." He touched the back of his head and winced.

"Is that where you got hit?" She walked over to him. "Let me see."

"There's nothing to see."

She pulled him toward her so she could get a better look. When she touched the lump, he flinched but didn't pull away. "That's a nasty bump you've got there."

"Yeah."

"Maybe we should have stopped by the hospital."

Jep

"Me? What about you? You refused to get checked out first."

"That's different."

"Why?"

"Because my legs are fine."

He pulled back. "And so is my head."

"Let me see your pupils."

"Em." He got off the stool and went to the sink to rinse his cup.

"Show me."

He rested the mug upside down in the sink and turned to face her. "You *do* know you can't tell anything just by looking, right?"

"Technically, yes." She searched his eyes. "But I was hoping it would be obvious you have head trauma, and you'd let me take you to the hospital." She looked a second too long and almost got lost. "They look normal." She frowned.

"You were hoping I'd have a bad concussion?"

"I *know* you have a bad concussion. You were knocked out. I was *hoping* I could detect it and convince you to let a doctor look at you."

He stepped forward, so she had to lift her head to look at him. "I feel fine." His words were rough around the edges and made her aware of every breath she took as silence engulfed them.

His hand reached for her face, and he ran the side of his thumb along her jaw. She inhaled slowly, smelling her aunt's lavender shampoo he'd used. It smelled musky on him. He was close now. Too close. A cold fear snaked up her spine, and she stepped back, clearing her throat.

"We should get to work," she said, lifting her drink to create a barrier between them. She'd felt that anxiety before, when she'd first found herself wanting more from him than she had any right to. She'd blamed it on his lack of faith, but that excuse was gone, and it left a hole she couldn't understand. "We don't have much time."

He nodded, looking sad and confused, but it passed. "Yeah. We should get started."

He took her cup and put it in the sink.

"We can sit in the garden. It will be nicer out there."

"Whatever you want." He turned and glanced at the fridge as he passed it. "What's this?"

He tugged a postcard from under the magnet holding it and turned it to read the back.

"*Arcul de Triumf*, Bucharest, Romania."

"They must not have taken that one," Em said. "It was one of her earlier cards."

"*The world is so big. I wish you could see it,*" he read. "This was from Jade?"

"Yeah. I thought Carla had given Lawson all the postcards, but I guess he let her keep one. She always wrote that. Same thing every time."

"I hadn't had a chance to look at them. Where was the most recent one from?"

"Uh, I think it was a temple in Cambodia, if I'm remembering correctly."

"You were always good with the details," he said. "I wonder if that's where the statue came from."

"What statue?"

"In the bedroom at the apartment. You probably didn't see because I knocked it over when I pushed the bed off the wall to block the door."

Em's head cocked to the side, and her eyes narrowed, picturing the room. "I do remember. I reached for it in reflex as it fell, then thought how ridiculous that was because we were about to die."

"You thought all of that?"

"Yeah, in like, a split second. You know how your brain slows everything down when you're in crisis. It was a figure of some kind."

"Yeah. A monkey man holding a knife up like this." He demonstrated.

"It was white." Her eyes roamed the room, looking at nothing as her mind put the details together, then she stared back at Jep.

"I know that look," he said. "You've thought of something."

"You got a good look at it?"

"Yeah. When I first cleared the room."

"Did it have flames coming up in front of the figure?"

"Yeah."

She swallowed. "I've seen that same statue before."

"Where?"

She didn't respond as her mind began going back over every conversation she'd had with Gardener.

"Em. What is it?"

"It could be nothing. Maybe I've got this all wrong. We can't jump to conclusions."

"Em."

"We need to get back to the office."

"Em, where have you seen it?"

"Sylvia Gardener has one just like it. Or, at least, I think it is."

"Your supervisor?"

"Yeah. I didn't really get a good look at the one in the apartment, but Gardener brought it back from a trip to Cambodia."

"She spent time there? Recently?"

"Yes, but it could be a coincidence."

"It could be. But it would explain a lot."

Em shook her head. "We need more. We can't accuse her of treason when all we have is a statue someone could probably buy at any market."

"We need to bring it to Lawson."

"Do you think he'll listen?"

"You're afraid he won't?"

"You two don't have the best track record. And we did just visit the apartment without telling him. Not to mention the last time I brought him something, he wasn't interested."

"You said information was missing from the files."

"I remembered wrong. Or…"

"Is that what Gardener said? That you must have remembered it wrong?"

"No, that was me but…I don't know."

"Is there anything else in her behavior that was suspicious?"

"She wanted me to report back to her and tell her everything we found. She was excited about me being

Jep

involved. I thought it was because she was proud of me." Her voice trailed off at the end, and her face fell. But then she remembered. "Jep. She was the only other one who knew we were going to the apartment."

Jep shifted into gear immediately. "We need to move on this now. I'm sorry, Em, but this doesn't sound good for Gardener."

"I know."

"We'll go back to the office, and I'll get a look at her statue. Confirm it's the same one. Then we'll go see Lawson. He'll listen. He's not a fool."

Chapter 23

EM FOLLOWED behind Jep as they stepped off the elevator.

"Where is everyone?" she said, looking around the empty office.

"It must be all hands on deck at the apartment." He headed to Lawson's office but found it empty. "Lawson's gone too," he said when he returned to Em.

"What do we do?"

Jep pulled out his phone. "Just a second." Lawson's phone went to voicemail. "Lawson, I need you to call me as soon as possible. Emery and I have found something. It's urgent."

"Emery!" Gardener called across the office. "Thank goodness you're okay." She hurried over, not looking at Jep. "When I heard about what happened, I thought the worst. I had to tell Lawson about what you did."

"That's okay." She knew Jep would have no trouble acting like they knew nothing, but her skin was crawling.

Jep

"He was...upset, but I thought you were in trouble or worse. I'm so sorry. I know I said I'd cover for you."

"Don't worry about it. You did the right thing. Luckily, neither one of us was hurt."

"I'm so glad I insisted Agent Booth came with you."

"I would be dead if he hadn't." She hoped Gardener couldn't hear the coldness in her voice.

"Were you able to find anything?"

"No," Jep said. "We didn't get anything. It was another dead end. The bomb destroyed anything of value."

"That's too bad."

"Where is everyone?" Em said.

"I don't have much in the way of details, but while *you* guys didn't find anything, apparently, someone else on the team did."

"Do you know what it was?" Jep said.

"I'm not sure, but listen, since you're here, could you have a look at something for me?"

Em looked at Jep.

"What is it?" he said.

"I've been going over some of the other information we've gathered, and I think I've found a link. I'll show you." She turned and headed back to her office.

"Should we go?" Em whispered.

"It would look weird if we don't. And I'm curious to know what she supposedly found. If she's trying to lead us astray, it's more proof of her involvement. And I'm perfectly capable of putting her in handcuffs until Lawson gets back if we need to."

"But what if we get it wrong?"

"I'd rather get it wrong than let her go if we're right. I've got no problem apologizing. Everyone already hates me anyway, so it wouldn't change anything."

He headed across the bullpen, and Em wasn't far behind.

When they entered the office, Em glanced at the statue. She wanted to see Jep's reaction to it but was afraid of drawing any attention.

"Here," Gardener said, handing Jep a few papers, and then she turned her computer screen around. "Our techs recovered some writing off a burnt file we found. There's a similar date there to other documents."

"Yeah, I see that. Any idea what it's referring to?"

"Maybe it's the date of another attack?"

"Could be. That was a good catch. Well done. Do we have any information about where it could be?"

"Still looking into it. You guys sure there was nothing at the apartment you can remember that would give us any clue?"

Was Gardener digging? Did she suspect them?

"No," Em said. "There was a journal, but we dropped it when we were making our escape." She looked at the statue again, and Gardener caught it.

"You like it?"

"Uh. Sure. I mean, not really. It's not really my taste." She laughed nervously, then cleared her throat.

"Where'd you get it?" Jep said

"An overseas trip I took recently."

"Cambodia, right?" Em said.

"You've always been good at paying attention to the details," Gardener said.

Jep

"They must have those statues in every market in the country."

"This one and about a hundred other designs."

"What made you pick that one specifically?"

Gardener lifted it and looked it over. "I don't know. I liked the look of it, I guess. Why are you so interested?"

"Just curious."

"You want to know what I'm curious about? Worried, actually."

Em bit her lip, then released it. "What?"

Gardener looked at Jep. "At first, I thought the idea of Em going out into the field was a good one." She rested the statue against her hip. "But then, for some reason, everything always went wrong."

"What are you talking about?" Em said. "Everything was going wrong before he turned up. Agents were killed. Files had gone missing." She felt like the air had been punched out of her lungs when she realized her slip. She should have let Jep do this on his own.

"What files?" Gardener said.

"Documents go missing all the time," Jep said, giving Em a warning look.

"You mentioned that to me before, Miss Chapman," Gardener said. "You asserted that you remembered the details wrong. Has something changed?"

"No," Em said. "All I mean is that Jep being a part of this team hasn't made things worse."

"They're certainly not better. We almost lost you today."

"Only because they found out that Jep and I were there."

"How do you think that happened?"

"I don't know." She looked at Jep, unsure how to move forward. She'd revealed too much, and now she was making things worse by trying to fix it.

"They could have been watching," Gardener said.

"Yes. That's probably what happened."

"If not that, then who could have told them? Who knew you were going?" Gardener's voice was steady. Curious.

"It's not something we can answer right now," Jep said. "We've got work to do, but thanks for showing us what you found."

"No problem."

When Jep turned, his hand moved to his gun, but Gardener responded first and swung her arm around. Jep caught it at the last second and ducked, but it connected with his head, and he fell to the floor, unconscious.

Em thought she had screamed but couldn't remember hearing the sound of it. Gardener shoved her back against the wall.

"Be smart and don't move."

"What have you done?" Em couldn't recognize her own voice.

Gardener shook her head. "If you had been satisfied to stay at your desk instead of traipsing around the city with Agent Booth, none of this would have happened."

"He needs a doctor."

"No. I don't have a problem if he dies."

Em thought she might throw up. "Please."

"You're a real pill, you know that? I thought you had

potential. I mean, you've always irritated me with that goody-two-shoes thing you've got going on, but I thought you would prove useful."

"How? I'm no one."

"Until Jep arrived and flipped everything on its head. Having you by his side I thought would prove useful. And all I had to do to get your full cooperation was give you a little positive reinforcement. It was cute that you thought I'd suddenly become your best friend. Unfortunately, you turned out to be a bigger problem than asset."

Em's stomach churned. "And this whole time it was you." Her mind spun with scenarios as she tried to put the pieces together so she could see the web clearly, but it was all mixed up. She *had* fallen for it. If Jep died, it would be her own fault.

"I really am that good."

"But you sent people to kill us. Me. You know me. You might not like me, but you *know* me."

"What was I supposed to do? I knew I wasn't going to talk you out of going, and I couldn't risk you finding anything. You're too clever for your own good, really. Stupid. But clever. That made you a liability, and the best way to fix that was to continue with the narrative we'd set into motion already. Agent dies at the hand of terrorists. It's been working for us so far."

"Us?"

Gardener smiled. It was the same smile she always had, but somehow now it was cold. Almost evil.

"So you *did* mess with the files?" Em said.

"Congratulations, you solved the puzzle, and the

only prize at the end of the rainbow is death. I hope you're satisfied."

Gardener took out her phone and made a call while she kept her eyes on Em. "Hey," she said to whoever was on the other end. "We have a situation." She listened for a second, then hung up.

"Why are you doing this?"

"While I was in Cambodia, I had a religious experience akin to—no, I'm kidding, but you should see your face. No dramatic religious zealotry here, I'm afraid. I am one hundred percent an atheist. But they do pay well, those fanatics."

"This all started in Cambodia?"

"Oh, no. This has been a long game plan. I've been working quietly behind the scenes for a couple of years now. Not from the beginning. There was a time when I had the ridiculous notion of doing good in this world."

"Did you meet my sister in Cambodia?"

"I did. Not too bright, that one. Desperate, though. Both of you. You looked to Jesus, and Jade looked to Mohammad. Both of you filling a hole."

"Jesus and Mohammad are not the same."

"Whatever. I don't really care. It all stems from the same place. What is it? Mommy issues or daddy issues? Because she was almost begging for someone to give her the love she never had at home."

"We all have baggage."

"Sure, but some of us deal with them in better ways."

"You mean like you?"

"As one example, yes." Gardener said

"You deal with your problems by assisting in the murder of innocent people?"

"I never killed anyone."

"You helped to do it."

"That's semantics. They don't tell me why I do stuff. They just give me orders and pay for all the nice things in life. It's a pretty good deal."

"You know exactly what you were mixed up in. You just don't care."

"Could be. By the way, out of curiosity, how'd you figure it out?"

"The statue. Jade had one just like it at the apartment."

"Did she? Huh. I had no idea. So you did get something good there after all. Too bad no one else will know about it."

"You won't get away with this."

"I guess that's what you have to say, right? It's written in the rule book. I'm afraid that real life isn't like fairy tales, Miss Chapman."

"Hey." Pearce entered the room. "I've been looking —" He saw Jep on the floor and pulled his weapon.

"Pearce!" Em said. "She—"

"He attacked me," Gardener said. "He went crazy when I showed him that we found information connected to when the next attack might be coming."

"She's lying," Em said. "She's in on this whole thing, Pearce. You have to believe me."

"After I knocked him out, Emery threatened me," Gardener continued. "She said they were going to rescue Jade, and she wouldn't let me stop them."

"That's ridiculous," Em said. "She's the one—"

"Everyone calm down," Pearce said, but he kept his weapon drawn.

"She knew about Jep and I going to the apartment," Em said.

"You were at the apartment?" Pearce said. "Jep told me he was alone."

"He didn't want me getting in trouble. I asked Gardener to cover for me, and then we were attacked at the apartment because she told them we would be there."

Pearce looked at Gardener, who scoffed. "You don't actually believe her."

"Yes, actually. But that doesn't mean I won't do my due diligence. Gardener, if you're telling the truth, you will be exonerated, but for right now, Emery's not the one holding the weapon." He nodded toward the statue, and she set it on the desk.

"I was defending myself," she said.

He pulled a pair of cuffs and tossed them to her. "Cuff yourself to the desk."

"Pearce," she said. "I'm not going to handcuff—"

"Now," he said, aiming a hard stare at her along with his gun until she complied.

"Fine. But you're making a mistake."

"I'll take my chances."

After she was secure, he went to Jep and checked his pulse.

"We have to call an ambulance," Em said.

"He's alive." He pulled a pair of cuffs from Jep's belt and cuffed him to a leg of the desk as well.

"What are you doing? He needs medical attention."

"I know. And I'll get it." He took Jep's gun and secured it in his hip holster. "But as much as I trust you, I have to do this right. It's still your word against hers right now. I need to make sure everyone's secure until I confirm what's happening."

"You going to cuff me to the desk as well?"

"No, you're coming with me."

"Where?"

"To check on your sister."

"She's fine. Jep needs a doctor."

"He's been hit harder than that before. He'll be okay."

"That doesn't even make sense."

He pulled out his phone. "Hi, I've got a medical emergency in Sylvia Gardener's office. Please send up a medic, but keep him cuffed. He's a suspect, and so is Ms. Gardener." He hung up. "Let's go."

"I'm not going to leave him like this."

"Em, I'm sorry. Someone will be up soon. This is too important. If you've been involved in Jade's escape—"

"I'm not."

"Good. The faster we confirm it, the faster we can clear all this up."

She looked at Jep. Blood was matting the back of his head. It was too much. His body could only take so much.

"Em," Pearce said. "Please don't make me force you."

She turned on him. "Pearce, you know me."

"I know Gardener too. Longer than you. Please. I've got a job to do, and I'm going to do it properly."

"Where's Lawson?"

"He's on his way back now. When he arrives, we'll fill him in."

Em looked back at Jep. "Once you know Jade is still locked up, we'll come back?"

"Immediately."

"Fine, then let's make this quick."

Chapter 24

PEARCE UNLOCKED the door to the room where Jade was being kept, and they found her still cuffed to the table.

"See?" Em said. "I told you. Now can we go back to Jep?"

Pearce sighed. "We can't."

"Why? You promised?"

"I know." He walked over to Jade and uncuffed her.

Jade watched him but didn't speak, just rubbed her wrists once they were free.

"What are you doing?" Em said.

"I hate to keep you in the dark here," Pearce said, "but it's for your own good."

"What are you talking about?"

"There's a lot going on that you don't know about. I need you to trust me."

"Trust you with what?"

"I need you to take your sister and find somewhere to hide. Can you do that for me?"

"No." Em's head was spinning now. She'd lost track of the twists and turns and had no idea which way was up anymore. "Tell me what's going on."

"We don't have time for this. Em, you've known me a while now. You know I would never do anything to put you in jeopardy. If you don't go now, your sister could die."

She looked at Jade, who quickly stood. "Are we getting out of here?"

Em's heart warred with her head. *God, you said to ask you if we ever need wisdom. I need it now.*

"Go, Em." Pearce said. "I'll cover for you."

"But where should I go?"

"It doesn't matter." He herded them toward the door. "You just need to go. Now."

"How will I know when it's safe? We can't hide forever."

She saw a flash of frustration cross his face. "Call me in forty-eight hours, okay? I'll let you know where we're up to."

She turned toward the door but was hit with a pang of indecision, and as much as she tried, she couldn't put a foot forward. "I can't."

"What?" Pearce said.

Jade took her hand. "Em, we have to get out of here before it's too late. Come on."

She let Jade tug her closer to the door, then resisted. "No. I can't. Not yet. Pearce, you need to tell me what's going on."

"You don't want to know," Pearce said. "Okay? Don't ask me to tell you."

Jep

"I'm in this deeper than anyone. I need to know."

His jaw worked for a second before he said. "Jep's the one."

"The one what?"

"The one who's behind all of this. He's been working for the enemy."

"No, it's Gardener. She told me."

A flash of anger appeared on Pearce's face, then disappeared. "Then I guess you were right. She was in on it too."

"She hit Jep over the head. She wouldn't do that if they were working together."

"Unless she got greedy and wanted him out of the way so she could get a bigger piece of the pie."

"Jep is not involved."

"I didn't want to believe it either."

"He would never—"

"You better be careful you don't let your emotions get in the way of the truth. I know you like him, but that's what makes him so good at what he does. Even I was starting to like him."

"It's impossible. He's only just returned to the team. He couldn't be behind everything that's happened."

"Did you ever ask yourself *why* Jep came back?"

"Because of you. I was there, remember? You put his name forward, and I went with you to get him."

"You don't know all the facts."

"Then tell me."

"Em," Jade tugged on her arm, but she pulled away.

"No. None of this makes sense."

"I don't want to drag you into this," Pearce said.

"Too late."

He growled but then said. "The only reason I asked to bring back Jep in the first place was because he reached out to me a few months ago. Said he wanted to come back. Begged me to bring him back. I told him I'd look into it. That scene at his place was all for show. He'd already made his decision. Em, think about it. He knows this agency inside and out. He knows how we act, how we think. He knows all our procedures. Why do you think he wanted you for a partner?"

Em wanted to explain, but the words that formed in her mind sounded ridiculous. "I've done okay. I've helped out."

"I don't mean to sound harsh, but you haven't. Not really. It was all Jep. Everything that's happened. Come on. You're a smart woman. He wanted someone he could manipulate and control. When you went to bring him back the second time, he knew he had everything he wanted. He had you wrapped around his finger, and I'm sorry for my part because I'm the one who sent you to him. If I'd known—"

"You've got it all wrong. He's not like that."

"I'm sorry. I know this is hard for you to hear. That's why I didn't want to tell you."

"Then what about Jade? If what you say is true, then why are you letting her go? All this means is she's working with him."

"I'm not saying she's completely innocent, but Jep set her up."

"And Jep's cuffed to a desk in the other room, so why do I need to get out of here so quickly?" As she spoke the words, fear crept into the tiny places in her mind and spread. Something wasn't right. As hard as Pearce was trying to explain, nothing he said could stand.

"I don't know who else is involved," Pearce said. "I don't know how deep this goes. I didn't know about Gardener. If someone else is connected and they discover their plans are unraveling, they'll start killing off the loose ends. Isn't that right, Jade?"

Jade's eyes shot to Pearce, then slid across to Emery. She licked her lips. "Yeah."

"You have to go now. This is your last chance. You're running out of time."

"Where's Lawson?" Em said. "When's he getting back?"

"We don't have time to wait for him. Go. Now. Jade? Go."

Jade turned for the door, but Em said, "Wait."

"Please," Jade said, "let's just go."

"No. None of this makes sense. It still doesn't explain—"

Pearce tsked, then pulled Jep's weapon and pointed it at her. "I was hoping it wouldn't come to this. Jade, come here."

"What are you doing?" Em said, as her sister obeyed with her eyes on the floor.

He handed her the gun.

"You're going to force me to take her?" Em said. "You're really that convinced that Jep is the bad guy here?"

"You have to admit," Pearce said to Jade, "I tried my best."

"There's still time." Jade said. But he shook his head and pointed at Em, and Jade lifted the weapon, aiming it at her sister. "Emmy. Let's go."

"No," Pearce said. "I told you. It's too late for that. I was hoping, Em, to keep you alive. You would have been a great witness. Everyone would have loved you."

All the heat went out of Em's body as the truth settled on her like a heavy dew, chilling her to her bones.

"You don't have to do this," Jade said to Pearce.

"Don't start getting all emotional now. You can't tell me you suddenly care about your estranged sister."

Jade scoffed. "I don't care. I just think keeping her alive is a better option. We've talked about this."

"It *was* the better option. Now, the better option is to say she was an accomplice. This wasn't the ending I had picked out, but you have to work with the clay you're given."

"Pearce?" Em said. "How could—"

"You ask too many questions. So, this is how it's going to go. You and Gardener were scheming together—Gardener is going to kill me for this. But after knocking Jep out with the statue in Gardener's office, you stole his gun and cuffed them both before coming in here to save your sister. Little did you know, she didn't want saving from you because she's been radicalized. She stole the gun and shot you before she escaped. How do you like that story?"

"You want me to kill my sister?" Jade said.

He pointed his own gun at her. "We could amend the story to—before you could escape, I shot you dead. Would you rather do that?" He clicked his tongue.

Jep

"Come on. Don't look so sad. It's all for the greater good, right? Right?"

"Right." Jade looked at Em before lifting the gun higher. "I'm so sorry, Em. This was never—"

"Wait," Em said, frantic. She should have taken her sister and escaped when she still could have. But the other agents would return eventually. Maybe if she could stall long enough... *God, please help.*

"Pearce," she said. "Why are you doing this?"

"Same reason Gardener is. Money."

They were good. She had to admit. Even now that she knew, she couldn't see it.

"You're the one she called from her office after she knocked Jep out?"

"Yeah."

"Then why the act at her office? Why pretend like you weren't involved?"

"Because that's how we do it. I wanted to keep my options open, and she caught on as soon as I entered and played along."

"Who was involved first?"

"If you're trying to stall, you're wasting your time. They won't be back for a while. I've sent them all on a wild goose chase. A master stroke actually."

"I'm not stalling. I'm just trying to piece everything together."

"Trying to figure out how you could have stopped it? You're not smart enough. We've put too many years into perfecting it, and you had no reason to suspect."

"It was Gardener, right? She was involved first?"

"Good guess. She knew about a few of my indiscretions and thought I'd be the right man for the job. It's been a long game, but it's about to pay off big time."

"What about Lawson?"

"What about him?"

"Is he involved?"

"Lawson? No."

"I didn't think so."

Pearce laughed. "And that's your problem, Em."

"What?"

"You're the kind of girl who likes to see the best in everyone. Even me. And don't even get me started on Jep."

"You don't know anything about him."

"Oh no? I know he's too righteous to play along, although he's made an excellent pawn without even knowing it."

"Why bring him into it in the first place? He's half the reason we found out Gardener was involved."

"That was unlucky. I brought him in because Truman was going to shut the task force down. Right when we were so close to our goal. Gardener and I would have been transferred to different departments, and we would have lost our momentum. I only brought Jep in to keep things moving a little longer. But it turns out he'll also make the best scapegoat. There are enough who don't like him and assume the worst, so it will be easy to pin everything on him. I'll say exactly what I said to you about him running the whole thing."

"You never called the medic, did you?"

"We're back to that, are we? No. I didn't. Whether he lives or dies right now isn't my concern."

Jep

"Gardener wanted us dead."

He tsked. "Yes. That was not my idea. I was pretty cranky about that, but I'm coming around to the idea of you both being dead. Your lives are giving me a headache. It's a pity. The public love to froth over the living when they think they're a horrible human being." He shrugged. "I did my best. Even at the apartment, I only knocked him out. I could have killed him then and no one would have known. I should have."

"And it's really only about money?"

"Very good money. If that makes you feel any better. It's nothing personal."

"I thought you were a decent man."

"I am. If you ask my friends, they will tell you I'm a really good guy."

"That's because they don't know you murder innocent people."

Pearce groaned. "Here we go. I'm not interested in listening to your rant on morality. So if you've asked all your questions… Jade, if you please. For the greater good. I've got things to do."

"There has to be another way," Jade begged.

"They said you were prepared to kill if necessary."

"Not my own sister."

"Jade, if you do this, they'll know you're serious. They'll know you are fully committed. Otherwise, it's clear you have not sacrificed everything."

"Like you can talk," Em said. "You've given up nothing. All you do is take."

"We all have our place. Jade, pretend she's someone else if you have to, but do it."

Jade closed her eyes in pain as she aimed. "For the greater good," she said before swinging the gun toward Pearce and firing.

But Pearce had better reflexes and fired too. Only Jade fell.

"Jade!" Everything in Emery tugged her toward her sister, but in the clarity of the moment, she caught sight of Pearce's shoulder dropping where Jade's bullet had hit him. With her momentum already starting forward, she shifted it and jumped toward him. After pushing his arm into the air, she struggled to reach for the gun, and another round went into the ceiling.

He swore and twisted his arm around, dislodging her grasp before he threw her against the wall, driving the breath from her lungs. She dropped to the floor and looked up at him.

"I liked you, Em." He had the gun pointed at her, holding it with two hands. "I really did. You were one of the pure souls in this place. That's why I preferred you to be a witness in all of this instead of a casualty. So I want you to know, I take no pleasure in this."

Em closed her eyes and folded into herself. *Jesus.*

Chapter 25

JEP'S HEAD SPUN, his eyes fluttering against his double vision as he attempted to insert his key into the lock on his cuffs.

"They made me do it," Gardener said. Watching him.

"Made you do what?" He squinted to make sense of the small hole when the key missed it again. "Hit me on the head? I don't remember anyone ordering you to do that."

"It wasn't my fault. If I didn't do what they said, they would have killed me."

"Yeah, well, you can save that for the courts."

"You've got to let me out of here. You'll never hear from me again. I swear."

"I think I'd rather have you locked up." The cuffs released, and his shoulders sagged from the exertion. He took slow breaths as he leaned back against the bookcase to give his head time to clear.

"I'm surprised to see you sitting there so calmly," she said.

"I'm dizzy. That's a heavy statue."

Gardener chewed on the inside of her cheek. "You're not the least bit worried about Emery?"

"Em's a big girl, and Pearce is doing what he's supposed to. It's what any of us would do."

"Ah, so you weren't as out of it as you appeared."

"With my head doing flip-flops, it was easier not to move. And I find you discover a lot of secrets if people think you're unconscious. Once he finds Jade safe and secure, we'll have plenty of time to unscramble the mess you've made."

"So you don't know?"

"Know what?"

"Uncuff me and swear to me you'll let me go, and I'll tell you."

Jep shifted forward, his head swimming. He blinked until he could see only one of her. "Tell me."

"Looks to me," she said with a smile, "like you're in no position to argue."

"I'm not letting you go. You're responsible for a lot of murdered agents, and you're going to pay for it. You're also going to tell us who else is involved and where we can find them."

"If I did that, they'd find me, and they'd give me a bullet instead of a paycheck. I can't have that. But what I can do is help you save Emery's life. If that's what you want." She leaned back against the desk as if she had all the time in the world. "But it will cost you."

He was impressed with her control. For someone

Jep

who worked as a paper pusher all day long, she steeled herself well. But even if Emery's life was in some kind of danger, he couldn't let Gardener see how much it affected him.

He moved onto his knees and used a nearby chair to drag himself up to his feet. "Tell me what you know. Did you put a bomb in the building?"

She held up her cuffed hand. "Let's trade."

Jep didn't have time to interrogate her, but he couldn't let her go, either. He'd have to bluff. "Fine." He pulled a chair over so he could sit close. Standing was costing him too much.

After unlocking her cuffs, he said, "Tell me."

"I'll text you once I'm out of the building."

He shoved her back against the desk. "No, you'll tell me why I should be worried about Em, or I'll break your fingers."

"Promise me you'll let me go?"

"Tell me!" he shouted and shoved her again. He must have looked wild because her eyes widened in fright. If only she knew how weak he was.

"Okay, okay. Back off."

He gladly sat back in the seat and took small breaths to keep the nausea down.

"Pearce isn't who he says he is." She had dropped her voice low, even though no one else was listening.

The sudden increase in his heart rate almost had him on the floor. It took him several seconds to regain his equilibrium. "Pearce is working with you?"

"Yes."

He punched the desk next to her head, and she

jumped, but he didn't give her time to react further as he grabbed her arm and re-cuffed her.

"Hey!" she shouted. "You have to let me go!"

"No I don't." He stood, knocking the chair over as he stumbled out of the room.

"You promised!"

He ran into a rolling chair and tripped across it, catching himself on a nearby desk. After righting himself, he weaved through the room, propping himself up on desks and chairs as he went. He battled the vertigo that threatened to take him back to the black hole, which could mean Em's death.

His hand skimmed along the wall when he entered the hall, and he fell against the elevator, slamming the heel of his hand against the call button. "Come on. Come on!"

The door slid open, and he fell inside. It took him a couple of breaths before he could crawl to the number pad and jam his finger on the floor number.

"God, help me," he said as he rubbed his fingers on his eyes to clear them. "I need your strength, and I need you to get me there in time."

When the door opened, he was on his feet, but he couldn't remember standing. He practically threw himself down the hall, hoping his legs wouldn't give way while his hand traced a path on the wall of the corridor. It seemed interminably long.

He could see the door ahead was open. Then he heard a weapon discharge, and he surged forward, entering the room in time to see Jade's body lying at an odd angle on the floor before he registered Em was

Jep

cowering against the wall with her eyes shut. Pearce was aiming his weapon at her.

Jep cried out for help from above as he leapt.

Em held her breath and flinched when the gun fired, waiting for either pain or the end. When nothing happened and all she could hear were muffled grunts, she looked up to see Jep hanging off Pearce's back with one arm around his throat and the other clamoring for the weapon.

The gun went off again, punching another hole in the ceiling. Em scrambled to her feet. She wanted to help, but all she could do was jump out of the way as the two men careened toward her and slammed into the wall. Pearce swung around, smashing Jep into it.

Jep was pale, and his face was tight, but he continued to hold on with his teeth gritted. Pearce flung his body back against the wall again, pinning Jep, whose eyes had rolled into the back of his head. When his arm went slack, Pearce wrenched from his grip and staggered free.

Em didn't know what to do as she watched Jep struggle to hang onto consciousness.

"Don't," he whispered. One of his hands was pressed into his knee, propping him up, while the other lifted in front of him like he could stop a bullet.

Pearce was breathing hard, but he held his gun steady. His eyes moved to Em. "At least now I have a good reason to shoot you both."

He looked back at Jep, and Em screamed as a shot rang out.

In the echo that followed, Pearce flinched like he'd been startled, then dropped to the floor.

Em stared at his dead body before looking to Jep for a weapon he must have been carrying, but he had listed sideways in exhaustion, his hands empty.

Her eyes travelled the room to Jade, who was lying on her back, her arm extended but resting on the floor. The gun was still in her hand. She was looking at Em, and her lips were moving wordlessly.

"Jade!" Em dove for her, but by the time she reached her, her sister's eyes had emptied and stared at nothing.

She held Jade's head and kissed her forehead, mumbling words of forgiveness and love as her tears wet her sister's skin.

"I'm sorry," Jep said from his place at the wall. "I couldn't save her."

"There was nothing you could have done." She kissed Jade one last time, then ran her hand over her sister's eyes to close them. "There was nothing any of us could have done."

She looked at Jep and saw he was in bad shape. Her sister was dead, but she couldn't let Jep meet the same fate.

She hurried over to him and touched the back of her fingers against his forehead. Then pressed her palm against his cheek. "You don't look good."

"That's not a very nice thing to say."

She laughed despite herself. "You need help. I'll call someone."

Jep

She dialed Lawson first, but he still wasn't answering. "Why is everyone still gone?" Her teeth were clenched in frustration as she called down to security and arranged for them to get paramedics on site.

She dropped her phone beside her and moved closer to Jep. "They're on their way." She wiped at the blood on his face but only smeared it. "You're not going to die on me, are you? 'Cause that wouldn't be cool at all."

He smiled weakly. "I think I can hang in there."

"Good. I can't lose anyone else."

He pushed up from the wall and grunted. "I should check Pearce's pulse. Make sure."

"No. Stay where you are. I'll do it."

He didn't resist when she pressed him back against the wall before tentatively making her way to Pearce's body, where she hovered over him, rubbing her fingers together to get up the courage to touch him.

"Wait," Jep said, holding out his hand. "Give me his gun. Just in case."

It was lying beside Pearce's hand, so she kicked it away before retrieving it.

"You sure this is a good idea?" she said, handing it to Jep. "Your double vision won't make you accidentally shoot me?"

"I'd never shoot you." His eyes sparkled a little. That was a good sign.

She went back to Pearce and lowered onto her knee. Knowing Jep had the gun gave her more courage. Slowly, she reached under Pearce's collar and grimaced as her fingers prodded his neck. She paused, then moved to another spot, just to make sure. "He's dead." She retracted her hand and moved back beside Jep, who'd dropped the gun into his lap once the danger had passed.

"Did you see that coming?" Jep said. "Because I am embarrassed to admit that I did not."

"No. I mean, maybe if I go back through every single interaction, there might be something. But nothing obvious. Gardener I can almost see, but Pearce?" She sighed, then shifted to get back on her feet. "I should wait at the elevator so I can show the paramedics where to come."

"Wait." He reached toward her. "Just wait. They'll figure it out."

"But what if—"

"Come here."

She looked at the door. It wouldn't be that hard to find this room. But she was desperate for him to be assessed so they could confirm for her that he would be okay.

"Em. Please." She moved closer, and he put an arm around her, pulling her toward him. "I'll be fine, but you lost your sister."

She hadn't realized how far she'd crammed that information away from any emotional part of her being until he spoke those words. Her body tensed when a fresh wave of grief hit her. She shook as tears poured down her cheeks.

"I'm so sorry, Em. I got here as fast as I could."

"I know." Her body shuttered, and she curled tighter into his shoulder.

Jep

"Whoa!" There was a shout from the door. Jep and Em looked up.

Agent Bailey stood at the threshold with his weapon drawn. "What's happened here? Is that Pearce?"

"At ease, soldier," Jep said. "The threat is contained. Have you seen any paramedics, by the way? They should be here by now."

Em wiped at her face but kept her eyes on the floor.

"What happened in here?" Bailey said, wide-eyed. "How'd the suspect get a weapon?"

"It's a long story," Jep said. "Is Lawson back yet? Where have you guys been?"

"I was the first to return. The rest aren't far behind. They're going to go nuts when they see this."

"But where were you all?"

"We were sent out to a farm in the middle of nowhere. Code red. There was supposed to be a whole nest of activity. Turns out it was abandoned but rigged with explosives. Good thing we checked first."

"We haven't been able to get ahold of anyone."

"Yeah, it was in a black spot. So...what happened?"

"You had better go get Lawson. And maybe give him a heads up about what he'll find, so he doesn't get startled like you did. I'd rather not get shot today. I've managed to avoid it so far, but my luck may be running out."

"I didn't get startled. Pearce is dead. And you're pretty calm about all this. You also haven't said what's happened to you. You look awful." Bailey shook his head. "Maybe I should stay here and—"

"Just go get him, will ya? We're not going anywhere."

"This is bad," Bailey said as he returned his gun to his holster. Then he ran his hand through his hair. "Poor Pearce. Man. As if we haven't lost enough good agents already."

"Yeah," Jep said. Clipped. "Now, can you please go get Lawson? I've got a headache, and I don't want to go through this twice."

"Yeah, okay." He backed out of the room, still shaking his head.

"Hey, Bailey," Jep said. "One more thing."

"Yeah?"

"Gardener is cuffed in her room. Don't let her go. She'll need to be questioned."

"*Sylvia* Gardener?"

"She's the only Gardener I know of."

"Why is she in cuffs? What did she do?"

Jep pointed at his head. "Knocked me out."

"Why?"

"Can you just make sure she's taken into custody?"

"You know, before you came here, this place was orderly."

"Orderly and full of traitors. Well done."

"Who's a traitor? Gardener? Jep, what—"

"I'll explain everything to Lawson."

"Okay, but make sure you don't go anywhere."

"I don't know that I could move from this spot even if I wanted to."

After he left, Em wiped her face with her sleeve and

sat back. "We saved a lot of people today, right? Jade didn't give her life for nothing?"

"If Pearce had killed us, there's no telling how many more people would have died. And when Gardener talks, we'll save even more."

"You think she'll talk?"

"I'll make sure of it. Your sister's death won't be for nothing. She's a hero."

Em let out a soft laugh. "That's a nice thing to say."

"It's the truth. But Em, be prepared. The agency won't look at her that way. They'll pick her life apart to find whatever evidence they need to condemn her and anyone else who will shift the blame as far away from them as possible."

"I know. But I don't care what they think. I know what was really in her heart. Underneath all her pain and anger, she could still do what was right. I only wish we had more time to explore that."

He tugged her close again. "I know."

Chapter 26

"YOU SURE YOU don't want to come in with me?" Jep smirked at Em as he tightened his vest. She rested her hand on the hard plate at his chest to confirm for herself that it would protect him.

"You know what would be funny?" she said, cocking her head to the side.

"What's that?"

"If I said I was coming."

"But you won't."

"Yeah, but if I did, what would you say?"

"I haven't had a great track record bringing you on missions. You've almost died every single time."

"That's being a bit melodramatic, don't you think?"

"Not when it's the truth."

"You wouldn't have let that homeless man kill me."

He leaned toward her. "That is very true. But you'll have a scar to prove my incompetence for the rest of your life."

"Stop being so hard on yourself. Scars are cool,

didn't you know? And it will remind me that someone believed in me enough to test my skills."

"That's generous."

"Would you rather I remember you as being careless?"

His eyes dipped to her smile, and he opened his mouth to speak, but Agent Cramer beat him to it.

"Jep. We're ready," he said.

"Thanks." Jep nodded, then looked back at Em. "I guess I'll see you on the other side."

"You'd better. Promise me you'll be careful."

"I always am."

"That's not true."

"You can pretend it is if it makes you feel better."

She grunted when he jogged off before she could come up with a comeback.

"I know Jep and I haven't always gotten along," Lawson said as he approached her, his hands tucked deep in his pockets. "But he's a great agent."

"He is."

"We operate differently, so we'll never see eye to eye, but after what happened with Pearce, I can see that bringing Jep onto the team was the best move we could have made."

"I'm glad to hear you say that." She rubbed her hands together against the chill in the night. "How long do you think this op will take?"

"Depends on what they find. They'll have to move slower than usual to ensure we don't have another event like the last one."

"But you trust Gardener's intel?"

"I think Gardener will do whatever is in her own best interest, and right now, that means bringing these guys down. If they're out of commission, she has a better chance of not being killed by them."

"I hope you're right."

"It's natural to be worried, but are you sure you want to be out here for this?"

"I'd go crazy otherwise."

An owl hooted nearby.

"I have to say, Miss Chapman." He was staring at the line of trees that concealed them. "You're not what I expected."

"I'll take that as a compliment."

"You should. We could use more like you on the team."

"You sure you could handle more than one of me?"

He laughed. "It's good to have some who think differently from the rest."

"If you really mean that, I would be happy to add a summary of my thoughts to the reports."

"Actually, I was thinking more along the lines of you becoming a trained field agent."

"Have you already forgotten the messes I've been getting into since going into the field?"

"None of which were on account of you and all of which you handled remarkably well."

"I owe a lot to Jep. I'm not sure if I'm cut out for fieldwork without him by my side."

"You've already been through more action than most people see their entire lives. And I'll admit, I thought Jep

Jep

was up to something when he chose you for a partner. Little did I know he saw what the rest of us missed. At least think about being retrained. Don't say no yet."

"I can think about it."

"Good."

Lawson's walkie talkie squawked, alerting him that the team was in position and ready to breach.

"We'd better get inside," Lawson said.

She followed him into the tactical van.

"Kay. Sylvestro." She nodded a hello to the two technicians she'd only met today. It was tight with all the equipment. Even tucked against the side wall, her knees kept bumping Agent Kay's chair.

"Sorry," she said, adjusting herself after bruising her knee.

"It's all part of experience," Kay said with a chuckle. "This your first time?"

"Believe it or not," Lawson said. "She's usually on the other end of these things."

"I heard." Sylvestro said. "You're quite the legend, Miss Chapman."

"That must be for my thorough analytical skills," Em said.

"On the field, yeah. I hear you have a real eye for detail. I prefer to do my observation on this side of the monitors." He tapped a screen.

"And I would never let you out there," Lawson said to Sylvestro as he handed Em a pair of headphones. "You can hear what's happening, but you won't be able to communicate. If you need to step outside for a breath, you can. Things could get intense, and I know how hard it is sitting on the sidelines."

She blew a breath of air up her forehead. "I hope I don't have to take you up on that."

Kay adjusted a few knobs while Sylvestro was busy on a laptop. Em slipped on the headphones to the sound of crackling, but no one was speaking.

Then a voice came through. "We're in position, sir."

"You are clear to breach," Lawson said.

Em scanned the monitors, unsure which one was Jep's. She didn't want to ask, afraid to interrupt anyone's concentration.

Lawson looked back to her. "Screen three is Agent Booth," he said as though reading her mind.

She tilted her body sideways so she could lean closer and squinted at the screen, looking at what Jep was looking at. She narrowed her eyes to increase her focus, like she could spot a threat and save him from it. Her thumb kneaded into her palm as he moved with the group deeper into the building.

Her lips moved as she prayed for them, asking for God's wisdom and discernment and any other words she could think of.

Then the camera lit up as shots were fired. Everyone in the van tensed.

Em could hear snippets of Jep and others shouting, but there was too much going on to make out most of it.

Her fist pressed against her mouth as she fought for calm, trying not to make a sound.

When Jep's screen cut out, she jumped to her feet. "What happened? What does that mean?"

Jep

"Hang on," Lawson said. "We can't do anything right now but watch and wait. It could be anything."

"Man down!" someone yelled.

"No." The word slipped from her lips.

"Emery," Lawson said in warning.

She examined all the screens, trying to discern anything about what had happened, but it was getting too hard to breathe. She tossed the headphones aside and launched out of the van, stumbling to a bush before she dry-heaved several times. She stood hunched over with her hands anchored to her knees as she spit out thick saliva, regaining her breath.

After everything they'd been through, this couldn't be the end for him.

She couldn't think of any words to pray, so she let the pain in her heart go up to heaven. When she heard more rapid gunfire, she squeezed her eyes close. "Please, please, please." She tried to rein in her thoughts, but it was harder than when she was stuck in the janitor's closet. Images of Jep's dead body lying on the floor pressed incessantly for her attention.

Finally, the firing stopped, and she looked out into the darkness, holding her breath.

"Emery." Lawson's head was poking out the back of the van. "Get back in here."

"Sir," she said, "I'm sorry. You were right. I shouldn't have been here. I can't—"

"Jep's fine. The building is secure."

"He's okay?"

"He did get shot, but his vest stopped the bullet."

She would have sprawled on the ground in relief if

she wasn't desperate to see for herself. As it was, she struggled to keep from cheering.

When she climbed back inside, she fumbled with the headphones, her hands shaking with a rush of adrenaline laced with fear and relief.

Jep's monitor was still out, but she could see in the others that suspects were being rounded up and cuffed.

When Jep appeared in someone's camera as it panned, a lump lodged in her throat. He walked up to the camera and held up a notebook with a map drawn on it.

"I think we've got something," said one of the agents. "It looks like we may have the location of several bombs."

Lawson stood, nearly bumping his head on the roof. "Armed?"

"That's unclear at this point."

"Do we know when?"

"No, sir."

"All right, people," Lawson said. "We need to move on this now. Cramer, you get that data uploaded. I'll get the bomb squad prepped and ready. See if you can get any more information from the suspects."

Em had to plaster herself against the wall of the van to let Lawson climb out. She continued to watch the screen until it looked like some of the team was returning. Then she climbed out.

A few of them passed the van, and she knew, as much as she wanted to pull Jep aside when he showed his face, he had work to do. Seeing him alive with her own eyes would be enough for now.

She rested her hand against her stomach and took a deep breath. It was a good ending. Everything tonight had turned out well, but when she thought of how all of their lives almost ended on so many occasions, she couldn't help the bile that rose into her throat. It would take time to recover from the whole experience.

More of the team appeared, carrying boxes and loading them into the back of an SUV. It would be brought back to base, analyzed, and catalogued. She'd be a part of pulling the pieces apart and putting them back together. Organizing the information into a readable report. And there would be no Gardener there to delete any part of it.

"I hope this op hasn't pushed you farther away from the idea of being a field agent," Lawson said on his way past.

"I was standing here thinking about how traumatized I am after everything I've been through."

"We train you how to manage that."

"I know. But I did lose my supervisor, so there's a position vacant."

"You want to supervise? Really? Even with the danger, I thought you liked being hands-on."

"Do you remember when I came to you back before that first explosion that killed some of our guys?"

Lawson dropped his head. "I do. But even then, what could we have done?"

"Nothing. Unless I had listened to my gut in the first place. And if Gardener hadn't sabotaged the reports. I think I can do more good behind a desk. Although, feel free to bring me in when the guns have stopped blazing.

I'm good with that. I just don't think my heart can handle much more of this."

Lawson nodded. "As long as I get to keep you on my team."

"I wouldn't have it any other way."

Jep jogged up to them, and Em held her breath. "Sir, we're conducting some preliminary interrogations." He glanced briefly at Em but kept his focus on his boss. "It looks like this thing goes deeper than any of us thought. There are several terror cells involved, engaging in what they're calling guerrilla warfare. Taking us apart piece by piece. Not a bad tactic."

"It worked well for a while."

"They've recruited a lot of US citizens. The ones they couldn't radicalize, they offered whatever it took. Money, power, influence. We're already compiling a list."

"That's good work," Lawson said. "It was well organized and executed. But for now, let's focus on the imminent threats. Do you have any more details about the bombs?"

"Two days is what they said. They're armed. I can go with Cramer. We'll head to the site—"

"No, we're evacuating the area as we speak, and we've got a team en route." He looked at Jep's chest. "Where'd it get ya?"

Jep tapped the bullet still lodged in the plate. "I'll have a bruise."

"You might have more than that. I want you to get checked out."

"It's not that bad."

Jep

"It's been two days since you were cleared of the concussion. I'm not taking any chances."

"Yes, sir. Then I'll head back and help out with the interrogation."

Lawson clapped Jep on the shoulder. "Why don't you take a beat?"

"I'm fine, sir."

"Still." He looked at Em and smiled. "We've got everything under control." He turned toward an agent who was passing by. "Hey, Farris," he said, leaving Em and Jep alone.

"You enjoy the show?" Jep said with a smirk to Em's frown.

"That was awful. I thought you were dead. Again."

"After everything we've been through?"

"Your camera went off, and someone was yelling 'man down'. What was I supposed to think?"

He slipped off his jacket and removed the vest, groaning as he pulled it off.

"Lift up your shirt," Em said, pulling out her phone and turning on the flashlight. The floodlights had been set up nearby, but she and Jep were standing in shadow.

"What is it you expect to find?"

"I want to see how bad it is."

He pulled up his shirt, and she followed the hem of his T as it lifted, not trying very hard to ignore the waves of muscle. She focused the light on the bruised lump near his heart.

"Ouch," she said, shaking her head. "That must have hurt."

"It did."

"You going to get it checked out like Lawson ordered?"

"That wasn't an order," Jep said, tugging his shirt back into place.

"What if you have a cracked rib?"

"Then they'll x-ray me and tell me I have a cracked rib and that I should rest."

"And you should. You should at least take a few days off."

"Don't worry. I'm taking more than that."

"Good. You deserve a break after everything you've done."

"Em." He reached for her hand but looked around at all the people. "Come here." He led her away from the noise. "I'm taking more than a break."

"What do you mean?"

"I was only brought back for this one job."

"I was talking to Lawson. He's changed his mind about you. I think if you wanted to stay, he'd be happy to have you."

"It's not that."

"Then what is it?"

He sighed. "It's the work I was doing back at the shop with the boys. I thought I was wasting my time, but somehow, through all of this, I realized how important it was. How much those guys need me. Otherwise, they end up in a building like this creating bombs or carrying drugs for someone who would shoot them if they made one small mistake. I need to go back there."

"You can't do both this and that?"

Jep

"If I'm going to make it work, I have to put everything into it."

She nodded. "I know you're right. Of course you are." She swallowed back the emotions she'd had plenty of practice ignoring.

"Besides, they don't need me," Jep said. "They have you."

"Very funny."

"I'm not joking. They now know what an amazing agent you would make."

"Lawson asked me about it tonight."

"About being a field agent? Great. I hope you said yes."

"No way. I can't take that kind of pressure. The thought of going back out there. Especially without you… Sitting at a desk is more my speed. And I can still do good work there. Maybe more."

"You don't want to go into the field at all?"

"Maybe on the odd occasion when the danger has passed, and I don't need you there to save my life."

An awkward pause filled the space like a vacuum, siphoning the essence out of everything they wouldn't say.

"Looks like God used these events to give us both exactly what we wanted," Jep said, looking at the ground.

"I hadn't thought of it that way."

"You haven't really had time."

"There you are," Bailey said as he hurried up to Jep. "We've got one of them on the ropes. He's gonna crack. You want in on this?"

"Yeah, I'm on my way. Go ahead. I'll catch up with you." He looked at Em. "I should—"

"Yeah, go. This is more important than us reminiscing about the times we almost died."

"I hope you'll come out to visit the workshop sometime."

"I'd love to…when I can get away from work. But things will be pretty busy for a while after everything…"

"Yeah, well…whenever you get the chance." He bit his lip. "I guess I'll see ya around."

She nodded as he jogged off after Bailey. The best thing she could do now was to say goodbye and be done with it. There was no point holding onto something that would never be. And with everything that was happening, the chaos of the investigation, they probably wouldn't see each other again or even have to say goodbye.

Chapter 27

EMERY LAID a pile of daisies across her lap once she'd gotten comfortable on the boulder beside her aunt.

"It's a beautiful day," Carla said. "I'm glad we're doing this."

"I wish we could have done something more formal."

"Jade would hate that, and you know it."

Em laughed. "She would."

"You understand why they can't release her body right now, right?"

"I do. But this doesn't feel like it's enough." Em leaned against Carla, resting her head on her aunt's shoulder.

"It's enough that we can come here and remember your sister for the good she did. And we can keep coming back as long as we want to."

"I loved this spot growing up."

"Even though you almost drowned here?"

"Maybe because of it. My big sister being the hero and coming to my rescue."

"Where did it happen?"

"Right over there." Em pointed upstream to a shallow area of the creek. "The water was higher then. I remember the rocks were underwater. And they were slippery. If Jade hadn't been here to save me—" She ran her fingers along the scar on her head.

"I wouldn't be sitting here with you right now."

"And she did it again." Em smiled sadly. "Right at the end. It breaks my heart that she didn't know Jesus."

"Well...we can't know that for sure. She came to church a few times. Who knows what decisions she made then or even right at the end."

"She hated church."

"I know that's what she *said*. But there was a Sunday when she had tears in her eyes. She didn't think I saw, but I did."

"You sure it wasn't the aftereffects of a yawn?"

"I can tell the difference. She had enough emotion on her face. She couldn't hide the truth. And don't forget, she went against everything they tried to fill her head with and—at the end—chose you. She could have reached out to Jesus in those last moments too. With her last breath."

Em wiped the tears, but more followed. Carla put her arm around her.

"She always did love you," Carla said. "She just didn't know how to do it well. You both had to protect yourselves, but you did it in different ways."

"If I'd understood that better, we could have been

Jep

closer. Maybe I could have kept her from being influenced like she was."

"She was an adult. You can't take responsibility for her actions. My home was always open for her to come back to, and she chose differently. Don't start taking on that baggage."

"It's strange to miss someone so acutely who you barely saw while they were alive."

Carla took a daisy from Em's lap, ran the petals across her cheek, then threw it into the water. "Goodbye, Jade."

Em threw in one of her own. "You'll be missed, but always remembered."

The two women sat in silence as they continued tossing the daisies in one after the other until Em held the last one. "You know why daisies were her favorite?"

"I have no idea."

"Because she said there was no point pining for something you couldn't have. Daisies are easy to find, so she said she could have some whenever she wanted. She never had to go without." Em threw the last flower into the water and watched it flow down to a rock where it got stuck for a second before the current swept it around and it followed the path the rest had taken.

Carla stood and swiped at the back of her pants. "Why don't we go for a walk?"

"Good idea."

They hopped back onto solid ground and followed a path that wound through the trees.

"The few times we came here together, even though it took a lot of convincing, we pretended we were princesses lost in the forest, waiting for our knights in shining armor to come rescue us."

"I didn't think Jade was the princess type. You either, for that matter."

"I think we did it to feel normal. Other girls played like that. Other girls with a mom and dad who loved them. Maybe we thought it would help us escape."

"Did it?"

"For a minute."

"Speaking of knights, you haven't mentioned Jep at all."

She glared at her aunt. "What is it with you and him?"

"What? I'm just wondering if you guys are still working together."

Em focused on the path ahead. "He went back home. He's got other work he's doing."

"What other work?"

"He has a workshop where he helps guys who have made poor choices in life. Helps them get back up onto their feet. Make better choices."

"You never told me that."

"I didn't know I was supposed to."

Carla stopped her. "What's going on?"

"What? Nothing. I told you, he's gone back home. The end."

"Does that make you sad?"

"Why would it?"

"Because he's a good guy. Perfect for you. He knows you better than anyone else, but he's not a Christian. You did what's best, but it's okay to be bummed."

"Actually..."

When Em didn't continue, Carla yanked her around so they were facing each other. "Actually, what?"

"Apparently...he is a Christian."

"Hold the phone, what? You mean like a real Christian?"

"Is there another kind?"

"There's weird ones."

"He's not weird."

"Why didn't you tell me?"

"Since when do you need to know everything about this guy?"

"Since you're really into him. What's going on? He's got the whole package. What happened? Did he come out and say he had absolutely no interest in you romantically?"

"No. He..." She was trying to choose her words carefully, but there was no careful about it. "I think there was something."

"What?"

"We almost kissed. Thinking back, it was probably more than once."

"What?" Carla threw her hands in the air and marched in a dramatic circle. "I can't believe I'm only just now hearing about this. When did this happen?"

"We were at your place and—"

"Whoa, whoa, whoa. Not only did he try to kiss you, but it happened at my place? Where was I?"

"Out."

"And why in God's name did it not happen? And I

can say that because I'm pretty sure God's in favor of you two."

"You don't know that."

"It's a pretty good guess. So what's the deal?"

Em started walking again. What answer could she give?

"He's not your colleague anymore," Carla said when she caught up. "Why are we even having this conversation? Why aren't you with him right now? What are you doing?"

"I don't know. Leave me alone." Em picked up the pace.

"No way. Not on this. You've spent your whole life hesitating, and you're finally getting some confidence, so what's the problem? Are you scared?"

"Why would I be scared?"

"I don't know. You tell me."

"I guess… He's everything I never imagined could be in one man."

"You're afraid he's too good to be true?"

"No, it's not that—it's—"

"What?"

"Well, who am I? I had all these expectations about the man I would be with one day. He probably has the same expectations about a future wife."

"I doubt he's put as much analyzing into it as you have."

"So? It doesn't really matter. Why would he be interested in a girl like me?"

"He must be, otherwise he wouldn't have tried to kiss you."

"But he still left."

"What if God wanted him back at that other job? He's supposed to go against God's wishes? Don't you want a man who chooses God over you?"

"You are so frustrating."

"Why? Because I'm right? What did he say when he left?"

"Goodbye."

"That's it? Did he invite you to visit?"

"Kind of."

Carla groaned. "You say I'm frustrating. What did he say? Exactly."

"He said he hoped I would visit sometime. But he was being polite."

"No, he wasn't. Let's get that straight right now. I can forgive you your ignorance because men can turn our minds into Jello, but what he did was leave a door open hoping—probably praying—that you would walk through it. I think you should go see him."

"That is a terrifying thought."

"You said you weren't scared."

"I lied."

"So? You've done plenty of scary things. Visiting the man you may be in love with is worth facing the fear."

"What if I turn up and he's disappointed to see me?"

"Then you'll know. Wouldn't it be worse to get ten years down the road not knowing? Every day wondering what would have happened if you took a chance?" When Em scrunched up her face in indecision, Carla said, "Look, if you visit him, and he's standoffish and isn't showing any interest, you can say goodbye and that's it. No harm done."

Em looked up at the sky, a pile of emotions bearing down on her. "I can't do this right now. Can we change the subject?"

"You're right. Our emotions are high today."

"You want what's best for me, and I love you for that. But I think maybe God brought Jep into my life to help me embrace the person He created me to be. I'm satisfied with that."

"Are you?"

"Yes."

"Okay. I'll let it go."

Jep hadn't laughed so hard in a long time, but this new kid had a way of bringing the best out in all of them. Even Slate. He could remember seeing something in Bryce that day at the park when he'd saved him from being beaten up by the drug dealers, even though he'd had him arrested. It was a lifetime ago, but seeing him away from all of that, it was clear now that God was calling the boy to more. And Jep had the honor of being a part of that.

The sound of someone clearing their throat had them all looking toward the front of the workshop.

"Em?" Jep said, his mouth dropping open. He closed it when he realized his heart might jump out.

"I hope I'm not interrupting," she said, hesitant to step in any farther.

Jep

"No. Not at all."

Bryce snickered, and Jep elbowed him but didn't take his eyes off Em. He'd thought about her a lot since he'd come back, wondering if he should have made himself clearer about wanting to see her again. Wanting more, actually, but he didn't want to push.

"I noticed you have a lot of cars outside waiting to be serviced," she said, taking a few steps and looking around.

"Yeah. We've had an increase in support. Probably because I'm putting more effort into it. You remember Bryce?"

"We know each other?" Bryce said, stepping forward with a wide grin on his face. "I'm sure I would have remembered." He pulled off his baseball cap and squeezed it to his chest.

"She's the reason you're still alive," Jep said.

Em looked confused. "It's nice to meet you, Bryce. I'm afraid I can't remember either."

"Sure you do," Jep said. "When you first came here and dragged me away from this place, you saw what was happening in the park. Those guys were about to give Bryce a beating."

"Oh, you're that kid."

"I'm not a kid." Bryce straightened.

Slate rubbed the top of his head. "Sure you are."

She looked at Jep. "How'd you manage that one?"

"I told him to give me a call if he wanted to change his life around. He called."

"Smart move, Bryce," she said. "I think you've got a lot of potential."

"What makes you say that?" Bryce said.

"You like to lift up those around you," she said. "That's a good quality in a leader."

"I miss this," Jep said. "Your insight. You're not looking for work, are you? 'Cause I know you couldn't possibly be here to recruit me again."

"I wouldn't dream of it. But you said I should come by some time, so I am."

He could see how nervous she was. That could mean she was here for more than a casual visit. His heart beat faster. "I'm glad you came."

"Yeah?"

When she bit her lip to hold back her smile and looked at the floor, his confidence rose. He hadn't come right out and prayed that God would send her, but of all the women he'd ever known, Em stood out as someone he wanted to be with more than anyone else. Spending the rest of his life with her seemed like a dream.

"I can see you ditched the work clothes this time." The skinny jeans and loose blouse looked better than it should have.

She lifted a foot to show off her sneaker. "I did learn a few things from you while we worked together, like dressing for the occasion."

"You look good." His eyes dropped down her body and then back up, catching her gaze flicking across to the boys, who were miraculously watching silently behind him. Probably because they didn't want to miss the show.

"Ignore them," he said.

Slate punched Bryce lightly on his arm. "Come with me. I wanna show you something."

"What?"

"Come on and I'll show you."

"I'm fine where I am."

Slate grabbed him in a headlock and rubbed his knuckles across his skull while he dragged him from the room.

Em laughed. "Are they always like this?"

"Always. If you want to hang around, you can find out for yourself."

"You sound like you need help running this place."

"I wouldn't say no to a feminine perspective around here now and then."

"It wouldn't be distracting for them?"

"The boys need training in how to behave around a beautiful woman. As you may have noticed." He may as well go for it. This could be the last chance he had with her.

"Too bad I already have a job."

He clicked his tongue. "Too bad. How's it going, by the way? You like being a supervisor?"

"Yeah. It's good. Really good."

"How's Lawson?"

"Same as usual, except that he asks my opinion now."

"Wow. He's come so far."

"And the team's running better now that Gardener and Pearce are gone," she said.

"As it should."

"Not as well as when you were there, but that's to be expected."

He had taken a few steps closer to her, but the hood of a car was still between them. "Listen, Em. This small talk is nice and all, but once you walk out that door, I may not ever see you again, so I've gotta be up front with you."

"Should I be worried?"

He laughed. "That all depends."

"On what?"

He skirted around the car and moved in. Close. She didn't move back. "I've missed you. A lot."

"You have?"

"Yeah."

"I guess we got used to seeing each other regularly."

"That's not what I mean. And I take it by that blush that you know it."

"Mentioning my blush makes it worse, you know."

He snaked his arm around her waist and pulled her closer. "What about this?"

"That's very forward of you."

"But you're not pulling away."

"No."

"Good." He leaned in and kissed her. Carefully at first. Tentative. It was a couple of seconds before her arms found their way around him with no more hesitation until the laughter started and some hoots from across the room.

Jep smiled against her mouth before he dipped his head to rest his forehead against hers.

"That's embarrassing," Em said with a chuckle.

"For them. Not for us." He continued to hold her close. "They mean well, even if they're obnoxious from time to time."

"We'll have to do something about that."

"Oh, don't worry. I've got plenty of chores to give them if they need to be taught a lesson."

"You think that's a good idea? Won't that make them resent me when I start hanging around a little?"

"A little? That's it? I'm only an hour out of town."

"Forty minutes from my place."

"That's not far."

"No. It's not."

"Then I expect to see a lot more of you than a little."

He pressed forward, moving her back to a more private spot and kissed her again.

Epilogue

"SLOW DOWN, BONNIE," Emery said to the three-year-old girl tugging on her arm. "You know mommy can't move very fast right now." She rubbed the top of her bulging belly where she could feel the baby kicking into her ribs.

"Katie has cucumbers!" A six-year-old announced from her place beside a teenage girl who was pulling weeds.

Bonnie ran to her sister and dropped onto her knees.

"The cucumbers," Em said, "had no option but to grow. Katie, you've been nursing those things since they've been planted. But where's your hat?"

Katie smiled and scratched her shaved head. "In my room."

"Jade, honey," Em said to the six-year-old. "Can you go run and get Katie's hat for her?" Jade jumped to her feet and sprinted for the house. "You're going to get a sunburn, Kate. That won't be very comfortable."

"I've had worse."

Jep

"That doesn't make it okay. But I'm glad I'll have cucumbers tonight for a salad."

"I told you, I'm on dinner tonight," Katie said. "You need to put your feet up."

"If I keep walking, maybe I'll get this baby to hurry up and get out. I'm tired of having to lever myself in bed every time I want to roll over."

"You still have a week until your due date. Be patient."

Em groaned. "Easy for you to say."

Jade returned and fitted the hat onto Katie's head.

"That's better," Em said. "Once you're done here, there's lunch at the house."

"You shouldn't be working so hard," Katie said.

"Making sandwiches is not hard."

"I'll be in soon."

"Come on, Bonnie, let's go see what Daddy's up to."

Bonnie skipped toward a large barn across a large yard.

"Keep up the good work girls," Em waved to her daughter and to Katie before waddling to the barn.

When she went inside, Jep was scooping up Bonnie. He kissed her before tucking her on his hip and carrying her over to Em.

"How're you feeling?"

"Uncomfortable. How're you guys doing?"

"Really good. I got another call today. Word's getting around the state that Slate's the best. Everyone wants him for their paint job."

"He's got a great attention to detail," Em said.

"You two must be related."

"I do love him like a brother, so that's got to count for something."

"It's lunchtime, Daddy," Bonnie said, head butting her dad. "I'm hungry."

"Lunchtime already?" Jep said before giving her a raspberry on her neck.

Bonnie squealed and slid down to the floor before running out the door. "Last one's a rotten egg," she yelled before disappearing.

"You could have called my cell," Jep said.

"I need to walk. Get this baby moving."

He rested his hand on her belly. "Three girls. What am I going to do with myself?" He leaned down and kissed her belly. "I can't wait to see what God has in store for each of them."

"That's a long way off. Let them grow up first."

"If I could have it my way, they'd never grow up. What am I going to do when the boys start sniffing around?"

"Don't worry about them," Slate said, ambling over. "I've got my shotgun. And you know I won't be the only one." He looked back at the workshop where three other guys were working.

"I can bring lunch out to you if you're busy," Em said.

"No way," Jep said. "I'll help you back to the house, then I want you to rest for a bit."

"I don't need help. Slate, you make sure they all wash their hands before coming inside."

"Yes, ma'am."

Jep

Jep linked his fingers with hers. "My hands are clean. I'll walk you back."

"You worried I'll go into labor on the way?"

"You never know." As they walked across the yard, Katie was headed for the house. "How's she doing?"

"Better."

"I hope those nightmares don't last much longer."

"We had a good talk about God after breakfast," Em said. "She has a lot of obstacles to climb over, but she knows it. She can see what her life's done to her, and she has a sense that there's more."

"She's turned up at the right time. If she can stick to this path, it will be good to have her around with the new baby. She loves the girls, and the girls have really taken to her."

"Yeah. It's sweet. But I do worry."

"About what? You think Katie could be trouble?"

"No," Em said. "But she could still go back out into the world and throw away everything she's worked so hard for."

"Like your sister? We knew going into this that we couldn't save them all."

"I know. But I can't help but wonder when someone new comes into our lives if this will be the one we lose. I don't know how God does it, watching us screw up over and over again."

"It's His long suffering. If you want to ask God for more, you know what He'll do."

"Make me suffer." She laughed, then stopped and pressed a hand to her stomach. "Oof."

"Are you okay?" Jep said.

"I think my water broke—" She felt the warmth run down her leg. "Yup, it definitely broke."

"So I was right. You did go into labor on the walk back to the house. Slate!" he yelled back at the barn. Slate ran out the door, drying his hands on a towel. "It's time!"

Slate went rigid. "The baby?"

"Calm down, you two," Em said. "I'm not pushing a baby out right this second."

"You were only in labor with Bonnie for two hours."

"Exactly. So we have hours. I'll call Carla and—"

"These guys can look after everything until she gets here. I'll get your bag."

Em laughed as Jep raced toward the house. He yelled to Katie, who stuck her head out the door, then sprinted onto the porch, launching herself before landing in a full sprint.

"You're having the baby?" she said, out of breath. "Now?"

"Not right this second." Em started toward the car.

"What do you need me to do?"

"Jep's going to have a heart attack if we don't leave for the hospital right away. Slate can look after the boys at the barn if you don't mind babysitting the girls until Carla gets here."

"Absolutely. Whatever you need." Katie's eyes were rimmed with tears. "This is so exciting."

Em took her hand and squeezed it. Katie had had an abortion not long before coming to the house. "You're going to be okay?"

"Are you kidding?" Katie said. "This is the best thing

Jep

that could have ever happened to me. I mean you." She laughed.

It was after she tried to kill herself that Jep and Em had been recommended to her by a desperate friend. Seeing her laugh was a gift.

"I've got your bag," Jep said as he swung it in the air. "Let's go."

Em hugged her kids before Katie took both their hands. Bonnie jumped, nearly yanking Katie's arm from her shoulder as she squealed in delight. Katie just laughed.

Jep led Em to the car and helped her into it before running for the other side, sliding across the hood to get there in record time. He cranked the engine over, and the wheels skidded as he stomped on the accelerator and sped down the driveway.

"Slow down," Em said, gripping his leg.

"Sorry."

"You can handle bullets whizzing by your head and bombs going off all around you, but when it comes to the birth of your girls, you're a nutcase."

He grinned. "I like to make the most out of life. It's more than I could have imagined, and if I want to freak out when my baby girl is born, I should be allowed."

"Okay, fine. But just make sure you obey the road rules. I don't want to have to call Lawson for a long overdue favor to get you out of a speeding ticket."

"Are you kidding? He'd love the opportunity, and you know it."

She grimaced as a contraction started. "Here we go. One more life coming into the world."

"What? Now?!"
"Just drive."

Jep took a deep breath, inhaling the sweet smell of his new baby girl as he held her his arms. She was gripping his pinky tightly with no intention of letting go.

"She's so beautiful," he said. "One more precious life to dedicate to the Lord."

"What do you think she'll be like?"

"Different from her sisters," he said.

"Sisters are always different. Even when I thought I knew our Jade and Bonnie would be unique from each other, I was still surprised to find out how different."

Jep kissed the tiny hand, then leaned down to kiss his wife. "How can someone have so much joy? God has been so good to us."

"All we can do is be thankful. And remember the good times when we have the bad."

"And never forget that God is always with us. Even till the end."

"Even in the darkness. Whatever we face—"

"He'll be there."

Enjoy the book?

Book reviews are the most powerful tool I have as an author to grow my readership. If I had the sway of a New York publisher, perhaps it would be easier to gain attention, but a simple reader review is way better than what any top publisher can offer…

Readers like yourself are what make the biggest difference to an author, and if you've enjoyed this book and wouldn't mind spending a few minutes leaving a review, it would help me out immensely.

Also by Shawna Coleing

Inspired by Judges Series

Contemporary Christian Romantic Suspense

SAMSON

GIDEON

JEP

JAEL

Hidden Alliance Series

Christian Romantic Suspense

HIDDEN TRIAL (book 1)

HIDDEN ASCENT (book 2)

HIDDEN DEPTHS (book 3)

HIDDEN CHANCE (book 4)

Want more of Peter Black? You first meet him in the Shadow Alliance Series below…

Shadow Alliance Series

Christian Romantic Suspense

SHADOW GAME (book 1)

SHADOW LINE (book 2)

SHADOW BREAK (book 3)
SHADOW TRACE (book 4)

Underwood Series

Christian Thriller
UNDER THE VEIL (book 1)
UNDER FIRE (book 2)
UNDER SIEGE (book 3)

Bristol Kelley Duology

A clean romantic suspense
SLEIGHT OF HAND (book 1)
SMOKE AND MIRRORS (book 2)

Erin Hart Duology

A clean romantic suspense
OUT ON A LIMB (book 1)
CUT TO THE CHASE (book 2)

About the Author

Shawna Coleing is the author of the Shadow Alliance Series. You can find her on her website or feel free to contact her by email at:
shawnacoleing@pgturners.com

Otherwise you can connect with her here:

Made in the USA
Monee, IL
05 October 2024